ERIMEM

THE BEAST OF STALINGRAD

Iain McLaughlin

THEBES PUBLISHING

ERIMEM

THE BEAST OF STALINGRAD

Iain McLaughlin

CONTENTS

THE BEAST OF STALINGRAD

THE ONE PLACE

Iain McLaughlin

PART ONE

Isabella:

When the cold comes, I think of her. Her eyes were warm. Her face kind. But in the cold I remember her. I remember her and I remember Stalingrad. Sometimes I ask myself if she was real. Was anything real? The war is over now. It is eight years since it ended. Eight years since we breathed again. Eleven years since those days in Stalingrad. Was it real? Did these things happen? Does my memory lie to me? No. They happened. It was real. Erimem was real. The terrible suffering we endured... the terrible things we saw in Stalingrad... those were real also.

Andy:

It's summer in Britain. That means it's chucking down rain and there's a gale howling in off the Atlantic. If Mary Poppins tries any of her flying malarkey today she'll wind up in Norway. Jesus, it's cold. If I had balls they'd be getting frozen off. I'm actually glad I'm working in the café today. When nobody's looking I'm giving the tea urn a cuddle to get some heat in me. I might ask Ibrahim to have a word with the new Vice Chancellor about the heating. It gets switch off at the end of April every year and we don't get another sniff of it until October. This – is – Britain! Summer here has a very on-off relationship with any actual heat.

Which raises this question: having recently spent a miserable few days in the pissing rain and mud of an ancient Greek battlefield, and then realising that summer in the UK isn't the same as summer in Egypt, why did Erimem decide to go somewhere even colder? I suggested we try London in the hot summer of 1976. That way we'd get some sun on us and I

11

could pick up classic vinyl I could flog for a fortune online. She wasn't having it. She hasn't got the hang of eBay yet. She knew where she wanted to go and I wasn't shifting her mind on that.

Is she stubborn because she was a pharaoh or is it just natural? And what's my excuse? I was stupid enough to say I'd go with her. Be interesting to hear what Ibrahim's got to say about this. Or maybe not.

Ibrahim:

They're idiots and I told them as much. "Stalingrad in 1942 is just about the most dangerous place you could ever go." Andy agreed but Erimem was resolute that she was going.

It was five weeks since we'd got back from Actium. Everything considered, it had been an interesting month or so. No, that's glib. I shouldn't do that. It had been a month that mixed a lot of relief that we were alive with the guilt that Anna, who had travelled back to ancient Greece with us, had been left there after she was murdered. It was logical. There was no way we could have brought her home and had the time to save Erimem's life as well. Still, seeing her family mourning at the remembrance service hit us all hard.

I know how hard it hit me. I'm a historian. Traveling to the past, to see one of the most important moments in the history of Egypt should have been the greatest experience for me. Instead it left me asking a lot of questions, mostly about myself. I came a hell of a close to dying myself because of injuries I got on that journey. Those injuries were inflicted by people at the university I had thought of as friends.

I trust people less now.

I trust myself less.

I killed someone. The Vice Chancellor of the University. He

had killed so many people and he would have been responsible for the deaths of billions. He was going to kill Erimem and Andy as well. I stopped him. A sword in the back. The logical part of my brain knows I did the right thing. I had to stop him and I did. Unfortunately, the logical part of my brain couldn't stop me remembering and it couldn't stop the nightmares. I had them almost every night. Nightmares about dying and others where I relived killing the Vice Chancellor over and over again. I don't know which was worse – the fear of my own death or realising that I was a murderer. Helena tells me it's natural, that my mind is dealing with it. She's a doctor, she should know all of this. It doesn't make me feel better, but whenever I wake from the nightmares, she's there beside me. I should shut up about her before I say something stupid and overly sentimental.

But I love that woman.

I was disappointed she wasn't as strongly against Erimem's plan as I was. But… she has always been in favour of people finding their own way in life, and since we had discovered Erimem's 'timeline' was what she called it, I think. Since we had discovered Erimem's timeline logged in the habitat's computers we had known Erimem would want to visit some of the places the computer revealed she visited at some point in her life. I just wish she hadn't chosen Stalingrad in 1942.

Andy:

I blame myself for Erimem wanting to go to Stalingrad. It was me who found that timeline of hers. Actually, the computer did all the hard work. It came up with all the places she would visit in her life, all the different times and places. It even gave names to some of them. She was interested by all of them because she could hardly remember any of them. We could tick off Actium and Alexandria. We knew she'd been there, but the others? The computer could tell us where and when she went but it didn't tell in which order or when in her own timeline it was. Were these places she had already visited in her personal past or places she still had to experience? She didn't have a clue and neither did any of the rest of us.

Erimem being Erimem, her first instinct was to pick a place and go there. She was curious about everything. It took a while to put her off the idea. We had to remind her of what had happened the last time we had all travelled through time unprepared. She didn't like it but she accepted the sense. At least I think she did.

She started at the University as a student – a student who got extra credit by acting as Ibrahim's assistant. That gave him the chance to keep an eye on her. It's really weird that she's his great great great… about a hundred and fifty-odd generations of great auntie. They seem to be okay with it anyway. Helena thinks it's hilarious. She is unbelievably cool with this whole weird set-up. I like Helena.

Erimem lives with Ibrahim and Helena now. Sort of. She lives in their airing cupboard. How Harry Potter is that? The difference is that Harry actually did live in a cupboard under the stairs – the cupboard door Erimem uses takes her into a sort of emergency escape habitat that's outside of time and space. Don't ask me. I don't know how it works. What I do know is that it's currently behind a very ordinary door and it looks like a villa from her home time with some modern stuff thrown in. I sort of designed how it looks – but whoever built the machines that control the Habitat were smart enough to know they should make it easy for idiots to work the damn thing. It was mostly just pointing the computer at information.

It felt like we'd all had a chance to stop and draw a breath after Actium. We'd been to the memorial service and somehow, we were all getting back to our normal lives. For me that included being the most hated person in my brother, Matt's life, for throwing his latest best friend out of the flat for smoking a joint. He hates me again.

Big deal.

He'd hate me worse if he wound up in the cells for a night.

I thought Erimem had settled to the idea of not visiting the places in her timeline until she rocked up to the café looking really determined about something.

"Tell me about Stalingrad," she said. "In the last century. In the time I was there."

I told her what I could. "Imagine Hell and then freeze it. A huge German army lays siege to the city in autumn and winter of 1942."

"It would be bad for the people who are there?"

"God, yeah," I agreed. "No food, no fuel. The question was whether they're starve or freeze first.

That seemed to make up her mind. "Thank you," she said and turned away. "I will need some very warm clothes."

I wanted to swear at her, but I was at work. It was quiet but there were a few of the new members of the faculty sitting having coffee. I didn't need them on my case. "You're going there, aren't you?"

She nodded. "I must." She was determined and I knew her well enough to know I'd be wasting my time trying to change her mind.

"When are you going?"

"Soon."

Honestly. What kind of crappy answer is 'soon'? If I ask my brother when he'll do the dishes, his 'soon' can mean 'never'. When a professor asks a student about an assignment 'soon' can mean 'three weeks on Wednesday'. I had no idea what Erimem's 'soon' meant. "Listen," I told her. "Tomorrow's Saturday. My brother is at some football thing until Sunday. I'll come with you."

She said no, and said I shouldn't... then she just shrugged and agreed to it. I had no idea what was going on in her head, but whatever it was, I'd have to dig the winter clothes out of the cupboard.

Ibrahim:

I tried to talk them out of going. I told them they were a pair of idiots. Bloody fools, both of them. They weren't listening. Erimem had made up her mind that she had to go to Stalingrad and Andy was determined to go with her.

Why Stalingrad in 1942? She wouldn't answer. She just said she had to go there and she would explain later. And then she smiled and asked us to trust her. Of course I trust her. Doesn't mean I don't worry about her. I said I'd go along with them. It was a close thing for who said 'no' first, Erimem or Helena. Helena won on volume.

I'm still not used to having Egypt on the other side of a door in the flat. I know it's not really Egypt and I know it's not really a door. All the same, I'm still not used to walking through from a first floor London flat to find myself in a perfect replica of a villa overlooking the Nile. Helena seems more comfortable with it. That surprises me. I thought she would struggle to deal with all of this. Andy seems more at home with it than either of us and Erimem treats it like it's the most normal thing in the world. By today's standards I had a privileged upbringing. You know the thing. Old family, plenty of money, good schools. I came out of that with a certain confidence. It's nothing compared with upbringing she had, and even when she's not confident, she knows how to project a sense that she actually is.

The confidence she had heading to Stalingrad was genuine.

If you watch her enough you can learn to read Erimem. I can also annoy her by calling her Auntie Erimem. At least she pretends to be annoyed. She was confident about this trip to Stalingrad, and she seemed to be driven. There was some purpose behind this journey. I thought about it and Helena and I talked about it in bed. We knew Erimem had gaps in her memory. Helena said it could be that those holes in her memory troubled Erimem and that perhaps making this journey to one of the places she knew she would visit would give Erimem more of a sense of control of her life. That sounded plausible enough.

"Do you think she should go?" I asked.

Helena snorted. "I think she's off her head to go." She softened her tone. "But I wouldn't dream of trying to stop her."

And that was that.

Andy:

I'd never felt cold like it. Five minutes earlier we'd been sweltering in Erimem's villa. Now, the layers of clothes didn't feel nearly warm enough. It actually hurt my face and I pulled a scarf up to cover as much of the skin on my face as it could while still letting me see. Erimem did the same.

We had arrived in a small street that cut off of a larger one. Well, I say street... is it still a street when half of it has been blown apart? The ruins of buildings were on either side. They were covered with a heavy layer of snow that smoothed the edges of the broken walls into hills. We were in the middle of a road but there were no tracks in the snow. Nothing had come through this street for a long time. There weren't even any signs of recent footprints in the snow. Of course, the snow was falling so heavily they'd have been covered in just a few hours, so maybe I was wrong. I didn't think so, though. The place had a feeling of being abandoned.

"Which way?" I asked Erimem. This was her show. She was in charge of this trip.

She looked around as much as she could. The snow was falling even heavier now. At a guess we could see fifty feet ahead of us. After she'd looked all around, she pointed along the street. "The houses seem less damaged in this direction." And she started trudging off through the snow. The way she moved, I got the feeling that she didn't have much experience with snow. Having said that, even when we had those bad winters back in, what was it? 2010 and 2011? Something like that? The snow was nothing like this. This just felt like the cold had been here forever. Walking was made even more difficult by the debris we couldn't see under the snow. The bricks and god knows what else from the wrecked houses almost did my ankles three or four times.

Maybe a hundred metres along the street it intersected another street. It looked bigger than the one we were in. Erimem had been right. The damage to this end of the street was nothing like as bad as what was behind us. The houses was all dark, though. I couldn't see lights in any of the windows. From the light – or lack of it – I guessed it was near dusk. If anyone was still living in these houses they'd surely have been some hint of light somewhere. There was nothing. I knew that a large part of the population of Stalingrad had tried to escape across the Volga. I also knew Stalin or his generals had put a stop to that. Apparently they thought their soldiers would fight harder if they knew their families were at risk. They might have been right but what a shit way to use people. But how bad must things be if they have to do something that shit to their own people? The ruins of that street behind us were a pretty good indication of how bad things were.

The street we crossed into was in better nick than the one

we left but just as empty. Still too close to the Germans, I suppose. We turned left and walked on a little. A shop with nothing in the window but signs that hung at crooked angles told us we'd definitely arrived in Russia at least. The writing was definitely in Russian letters. Cyrillic, they call that alphabet, I think. No idea what they said.

We had walked maybe another hundred metres when Erimem stopped. She brushed the snow off her woolly hat and pulled it up so her ears were uncovered.

I asked, "What is it?"

She didn't need to answer. I heard them coming a few seconds later. A sort of whistling, whining sound, getting louder. I'd seen enough TV and films to know what the noise meant. "Shit. Artillery shells. Get down."

I threw myself face down into the snow, grabbing Erimem and taking her with me. We'd hardly hit the ground when one of the missiles hit a house about thirty metres away. I can't explain how loud it was. You felt the volume as much as heard it. It shook us through to our bones. Even through the snow we could feel the ground vibrating from the impact. The missiles kept coming in. We could hear them getting louder as they got closer and then the explosions. We felt the blasts from the rockets exploding. The air a weird mixture of cold and then hot before it was freezing again. It whipped and caught at our clothes as we lay there, waiting for the bombing to stop. I'm not sure how long it lasted. It felt like hours but it was probably only a minute or ninety seconds. The impacts sounded further away and then they stopped. We waited where we were, in case it started again but nothing came. You could tell it was over. Everything was quiet again except for that strange sound of large flakes of snow landing on more snow.

When we looked up the winds that whipped the blizzard had blown a lot of dust and muck away. The house that had been hit first was a ruin. The roof was almost totally gone, the walls had huge holes and bulged out like they were pregnant. They'd collapse before long. Smoke was trailing up from inside. It was struggling to be seen in the blizzard. We struggled to our feet. The blast had left us shakier than I'd expected. We started along the street and I heard Erimem call out.

"There." She was pointing and then running as best she could on that awful ground. I need to wait for the snow to clear a bit before I could see what she was running towards. A woman was staggering away from one of the buildings near the one that had been bombed. She didn't seem to have a clue what she was doing. Her knees looked unsteady and she dropped to the snow just before Erimem got to her. I arrived not far behind Erimem who was looking at this woman with an odd mix of fascination and concern. I checked the woman's wrist. Her pulse was strong and steady.

"She's definitely alive," I said. "But she won't be if she lies about out here much longer."

We examined her as much as we could. She was maybe twenty or twenty two. She could have been younger or older, it was hard to tell. She looked more dead than alive but that was down to the way hunger had make her face too thin and lack of proper nutrition had left her skin grey. At least there didn't seem to be any fresh cuts or scrapes on her. "I think she was probably caught by a bit of the shockwave," I told Erimem. "She's been lucky."

Erimem nodded, looking around. "We must get her out of this snow before she freezes."

The woman's eyelids moved and she moaned. "She's coming around."

Her eyes opened and she tried to focus on us for a second.

And then she started screaming.

Isabella:

It will sound like a foolish thing now, but when I became aware again, I saw only this large, bulky shape over me. I thought it was a bear or perhaps something worse. But then I can hear her voice. A gentle, kind voice, telling me I would be all right. And this face, the same age as me, darker and from far away but filled with concern. And for that second, I believed that it would be all right.

But then I hear the shelling. The German guns blasting the city, same way they had for months. Many of us were now deaf to the bombs. They were part of the background every day. Like people talking or moving in the street outside. When I heard the shelling this day I was remembered – reminded – of why I was outside.

"I must go," I said and I tried to rise but my legs were not strong. The woman – with the kind face – said that I had been badly shaken. Her friend said I should listen to Erimem. I did not know these women but I believed that they would do me no harm. They helped me to stand. Erimem – the one with the darker skin – told me I should not be out in weather like this. That it was as dangerous as the shelling.

"What choice do I have?" I answered. "I must go home now."

But still my legs would not obey me and I felt both of these women support my arms.

"You had better let us help you," the younger woman said.

I did not have the energy to argue. I nodded agreement and let them help me.

Andy:

She was pretty shaken up. I held her up by one arm while Erimem was on the other side supporting her. Jesus, she hardly weighed anything. Any bulk she seemed to have was down to the layers of clothes she was wearing. She gave us directions through the streets, going left and right until we got to a wrecked building that looked like it had just come down. There was a much lighter dusting of snow on the rubble. The woman made us stop.

"Is this your home?" Erimem asked.

The woman shook her head, knocking clumps snow free from her head. "Wood," she said. "There is wood in the rubble. Help me."

She wouldn't go any further until we collected as much wood from the broken building as we could carry. We had bits of smashed furniture, broken floorboard and a few long thick pieces that looked like they might have been part the structure of the building, the spars wall panels were nailed on to. The woman had perked up at the sight of all the wood. Having two people to help carry it was a bonus to her.

"What do you want the wood for?" I asked.

"There is no fuel in Stalingrad," she explained. "This will warm my house for many days." She looked at me in puzzlement. "How is it you do not know this about fuel?"

Erimem answered. "We are new to your city. We arrived only today."

"I knew you were not from Stalingrad," the woman answered. "You are too healthy."

We went on a few streets. The damage was a lot less noticeable here. There were a few damaged buildings and some with random bullet holes in them but nothing nearly as major as what we had seen earlier. Apparently it meant we were getting closer to the river, whatever that had to do with it.

Her house was up a set of stairs in a street that had hardly been hit. It was freezing inside. Maybe even colder than outside. She started breaking up some of the wood to start a fire.

Both Erimem and I took the wood from her and used a small axe she kept by the fire to break up the wood. "Here, let us do that."

"Thank you. You are both very kind." It sounded like she wasn't used to people being kind. She started with the kindling and sparked a few flames in the heart. While I got the fire started, she told us her name was Isabella. She filled a kettle with water from a metal jug but she had to break the ice on top of the jug to get to the water.

"I can give you only tea," she said. "I have no food to share."

She sounded embarrassed but Erimem wasn't having any of it. She started rummaging in the rucksack she had been carrying. I hadn't given much thought to the rucksack. I had assumed it would be weapons or a first aid kit or something for emergencies. Instead it was full of food. She pulled out a pile of quick foods like cup-a-soups and those pasta and sauce things you just add water to. She had a load of them, then put fruit on top of them. A couple of apples and bananas. She finished it with a couple of biscuits and a few bars of chocolate. She pushed them all towards Isabella. "Take this. If you add hot water to these packets they will make food. The taste is not always good but it will keep you alive."

It was as if she was handing over gold. God knows the last time she had seen that much food. "I cannot take this from you," she said softly. "It is too much."

"Of course you can take it," Erimem told her. "Andy and I ate earlier. You will make good use of these."

Isabella gathered the food together. "Thank you. I can say no more than thank you."

She hurried away to make tea. I think it was so we wouldn't see how emotional she was. A bit of kindness when the world around you is so shit... I think it got to her.

I turned to Erimem. "All that food you brought... how did you know to bring it?"

She gave me a Mona Lisa smile. "Google?"

"My arse." I snorted. "Did you know we'd meet Isabella?"

Erimem leaned forward conspiratorially. "I will tell you later." So she knew something but she wasn't sharing. That didn't make me feel any more comfortable and she knew it. She smiled. "Believe me, I think this is the best thing."

I didn't like it but I agreed. A few minutes later, Isabella was back with tea. "Thank you for building the fire. You may remove your coats if you wish."

Erimem turned her attention to our host. "Now," she said. "Will you tell us why you were out in that terrible weather.

Isabella put hot tea in front of us and told us her story.

I am Isabella Zemanova and I am 22 years old. This is not my house. My parents lived here until some months ago. They were among the few who evacuated across the Volga, when news came that the Germans were coming here. Before Stalin gave the order that the public must stay. The army will fight harder because the public stay. I would not have left anyway. I left Stalingrad when I married Lev. He was a schoolteacher in Kotelnikov, a town west from here. It should have been good. Should have been happy. I love my husband very much. He is tall and strong but gentle and kind. There was talk of war with Germany, but Stalin signed papers with Hitler and we thought we were saved from this. But Lev knew. Lev knew that Hitler could not be trusted. I remember the day he told me that Germany had invaded our soil. Such sadness that he was right. That day he told me that we were coming to Stalingrad. That I would stay with my parents here. That they could help me care for our sons. We have two sons. Twins. Not yet one year old.

And Lev told me that he would enlist in the Red Army. He did this. He is educated. They made him a captain. He used this rank to find us food and fuel. He heard that the evacuation would stop and arranged for us to leave before this happened. But I would not leave him. He is my husband. When we first arrived, he would come three or four days each week. As the Germans came closer, that became twice in a week or once. But now it is two weeks, almost three since I have seen him. Erimem, you will tell me that in time of war a man cannot leave his post for his family. I know this and that is why I went to search for him at his post. He was not there. At first they would tell me nothing but then I see his friend Yuri. He told me that Lev was on special mission. Some days pass and I still do not see Lev. Again I saw Yuri. He was afraid. Not afraid like a soldier. Afraid of something more than the Germans. He told me a story, like a story we would tell children. He tells me that the dead are not safe. We are at war, surrounded by death, but even for the dead there is no peace, no rest. There are many dead in this city. We have no time and no room to bury them all as they should be. Instead they are stored and buried together, hundreds in one grave. Until then they are kept in old factories, warehouses, anywhere that is big enough and still standing. This was when I saw real fear with Yuri. The dead are not safe in those places. The bodies were going missing from these stores. Not all, but many. And others... they were cut, parts of them missing. I know there are cannibals in our city. We talk of them only quietly but we know they exist. I told Yuri this, that cannibals have done this terrible thing. But he knows I am wrong. What is doing this had been seen. A grey demon tearing the flesh of the dead. In the night, my husband Lev and his soldiers saw a figure, eating one of the dead. It ran when they fired their guns. Lev was sure it was a German soldier, driven to eating the dead by hunger. But the soldiers were closer. They said it was a demon. Lev does not believe in demons, Erimem.

He has learning. He set a trap for this demon at another place where the dead are held. The next morning, three of Lev's soldiers are found. They have been torn to pieces, parts of them eaten, the marks of bites tearing through their skin and bone as if a beast has attacked them. And Lev... my husband... of Lev there was nothing. None of his clothes, no sign that he had been attacked. Yuri swears that the army do not know what has happened to him. And so I search for him. Each day I search the city, looking for a sign that my husband is alive and will come back to us. I thought, perhaps he is searching for this German soldier who is eating the dead. Because I do not believe in demons either, my friends. I am not a peasant. I do not believe in demons or monsters... but if I do not believe in monsters then I do not believe in my own eyes, because I have seen it. With my own eyes, I have seen the demon that hides in the snow to eat our flesh.

Andy:

Yeah, that caught Erimem's interest quickly enough. "You have seen it?" She had questions for Isabella. Where had she seen it? What did it look like? How did it move? How tall was it? How many arms did it have? There were some really bizarre questions in that barrage. Erimem could get really carried away when her mind was on something.

Isabella gave us a few details. It had been a few days earlier, and she had been out in the city, talking to people she knew. Old friends, family... that kind of thing. None of them had seen Lev. Neither had Yuri. But they had seen somebody. Something. A spirit, some of them called it. The more superstitious called it something much worse. They said it was a demon. They said it was grey and it disappeared into the night like it was part of the darkness. Some called it Chort, the demon who eats children.

Erimem was leaning forward intently, demanding an answer. "But what does it look like?"

Isabella didn't tell her straight away. She took a moment to compose her thoughts then went back to her tale.

Isabella:

Night was coming. It was colder. Sometimes it is hard to believe it can grow even colder. But it can. Every night, it can. There was a street. Lev knew people who lived there but they had not seen him. It was late... dusk. I had been foolish. I had little time before it would be dark. I hurried as fast as I could but it is impossible to be fast when the ground is broken and covered with snow and ice. It was almost dark and I saw ahead of me a figure kneeling. I could see only a shape. But it was wrong. How it moved. How the head sat on the neck. Too high. And then a German shell exploded only one street away and it ran. Thin legs, not human. Grey and like wet leather. Its head was shaped almost like the helmet of a German soldier. Except it was bone. It did not see me and I did not see its face. But I saw what it had done. A man – I did not know him – this creature had been eating him.

Andy:

I can remember to this day the look on her face but I'll never describe the horror or the disgust in it well enough. She finished her story, telling us that she ran home, tripping over stones and slipping on the ice. And it made her more desperate to find her husband.

"Only Lev can protect us from this things. Only Lev can save my boys from this thing."

"Thank you for telling us all of that." Erimem squeezed Isabella's hand. "I know it is not easy to talk of such bad memories. That was very brave of you. Now I think you should eat something." She picked up a packet of pasta and handed it over to Isabella. "Put that in a dish, add two cups of boiling water and stir for a few minutes." You could tell Isabella wasn't impressed when she opened the packet and a clump of wee hard shapes and a sprinkle of powder dropped into a bowl but Erimem nodded encouragingly so Isabella went on with it. Erimem took the chance to lead me away.

"You can't believe it's a demon," I said.

She fixed me with a slightly accusing stare. "As you did not believe in the demon Ash-Ama-Teseth or travel through time?"

That was fair enough, but I had to argue just a bit. "Ash-Ama-Teseth wasn't technically a demon but fair enough, point taken. Do you have any idea what this is?"

"I know some things," Erimem said quietly. "Things I should not know, so I cannot yet share them."

"Can you explain any of that?" I asked.

"Yes," Erimem smiled wryly. "But not yet. I know that it very frustrating for you but I will tell you everything I know as soon as I can."

Erimem's expression changed like a flash when Isabella came across to us. She wouldn't hear of us going out in the night and told us we'd stay the night. Personally I was in favour of heading back to the twenty first century and my own bed but Erimem was quick in accepting Isabella's invitation. All this talk of some Russian bogeyman had her interested. And she knew something about it but she wasn't sharing. She was right. It was bloody frustrating.

Isabella went to her neighbour and collected her children. They were two adorable little boys. You should have seen Erimem with them. To start with, she was so panicked you'd think she'd been handed hot coals. They really took to her and wouldn't leave her alone. In the end she gave in and let them climb all over her she. Even sang them a couple of songs she remembered from her home in Thebes. When the boys were asleep we talked some more with Isabella. When she told us about what this war had done to her city, I wondered how anybody could have lived here.

Her reply was simple. "There is only one alternative to living, Andy. I choose to live."

I just wondered how long she'd have to live with the city in this kind of state.

We all had to sleep in the one room. If she was going to make her supply of wood last, Isabella said she could only heat one room. I could see the sense in that, so it was fair enough. I'll admit things have been tight enough over the last couple of years that I thought of doing the same. Working in a café doesn't pay much but somehow we always just about get by. Sitting there in Isabella's room, I was actually taken back to winters at my grandad's old house. He had an open fire and just wouldn't get rid of it. In winter I used to fall asleep on his knee while he read me stories. I was just dozing, dreaming of those old times when I heard somebody moving. It was Erimem. Somehow I'd known she wouldn't stay still the whole night.

She noticed that I was awake and pushed a hand gently down on my shoulder. "Go back to sleep, Andy. I am just going out for a short while."

"Looking for that grey demon, more like." She didn't deny it. "Well, give me a minute and I'll be right with you."

But she was already at the door and gone before I could even get out from under my blanket. I hurried to the window and I could just make out the shape of Erimem's dark coat moving against the glare of the snow.

"You are going after her." Isabella's voice came from behind me. I damn near leaped out of my skin.

"I have to," I said, reaching for my coat. "She's my friend."

Isabella nodded her understanding. "When you find her, bring her back here. You are both welcome here always."

I thanked Isabella and made my way out of the house, following after Erimem.

Isabella:

She left quietly, to be sure she did not wake my babies. I did not know if I would see Andy or her friend again. It was like this. Every time I saw someone, it could be the last time. It was living in fear, always. But we learned to live with it. I think when we realised that death was so much part of our lives every day, that was worse. Because we stopped fearing that we would not see people again and accepted it. We accepted death. We expected people to leave us and mourned less when they died. And we did not see that we died a little inside every time we did not mourn. But I knew that I would mourn Erimem and Andy if they did not return. They were not of Stalingrad. They had hope and kindness in their eyes. The cold had not frozen their spirits. I hoped that they would return. I hoped but did not expect.

My boys slept, the fire still burned. We were warm and we were fed. I went back to sleep.

Andy:

It was easy enough to follow Erimem. I'd seen the direction she took and there had been more fresh snow fall so her footprints were easy to track in the soft, fresh covering of it. She was the only one daft enough to be out so late in weather that bad. Yep. And that made me the only one who'd be daft enough to be following her. Which one of us was dafter?

I could see well enough. The snow gave a kind of a glow. That way snow does. It reflected that glow the snowy clouds have. I thought I'd catch Erimem quickly enough but every time I turned a corner there was still no sign of her in the street ahead. So I kept following her footprints. For some reason I found the tune of Good King Wenceslas running through my head.

I'd lost all the feeling in my feet by the time I finally caught up with Erimem. She was crouching at the wall of a shed beside a big industrial-looking building and she wasn't pleased to see me. Not a bit.

"Andy, I told you to stay behind!" she hissed at me.

"Calm down," I whispered back. "I'm only here to help. There's no point in me being here if I let you wander off on your own."

She shushed me. "It cannot be helped now. Just follow me – and be as quiet as you can."

We crept towards the big building. A door at the side wasn't locked and we went inside. It was so cold I had lost the feeling in my hands and my face was stinging. I'm glad I couldn't smell anything. It was just one big room and most of the windows high on the walls were smashed letting the snow blow in. But they let in what light came from outside as well. In the middle of that great room was a pile of bodies. Hundreds. Maybe more, all piled higher than our heads. Some were wearing uniforms and had been shot. Some of them had open eyes and mouths. It was like they had been stopped in the middle of talking. Others had looks of shock or pain. Those poor sods must have had time to feel the pain and know they were going to die. There were other people as well. Women, old men, even children. It was a place where the city dumped its dead. I was going to say something but Erimem held up her hand. Then she pointed across the room. Yes, sure enough, I could hear something. Something moving. Something breathing. Erimem gripped my arm and crept along the side of this stack of bodies. We got to the corner and she reached inside her coat. A *gladius* sword caught the dull light. It was a souvenir from our trip back to ancient Greece, and weapon she felt comfortable holding in her hand. We moved so we could see what was making the noise. What was round the corner... I'd never seen the like. It was Isabella's demon, just as she'd described it. It was as tall as a man but with thin, bony arms and legs and covered in a leathery-grey skin that looked wet and sick. Its head was round and looked like it was some kind of grey bone. Oh, but the face. Dark eyes sunk under a big boney ridge, two black holes where a man's nose would be. And the mouth filled with sharp teeth. Sharp like needles and tearing into the body of a dead soldier. It was eating the dead.

Erimem took a deep breath and gripped her *gladius* tighter. She was going to march out there and confront this beastie but it heard her breath and turned. You could see the flesh hanging from its mouth and it let loose this terrible scream. It was like we were looking at the devil.

PART TWO

Iain McLaughlin

Ibrahim:

I was on edge more or less from the moment Erimem and Andy disappeared from the Habitat. I read the controls twice and double checked that they had both taken the rings they would need to bring themselves back. It was stupid. They're both intelligent and resourceful. I just didn't like having no way to affect what was happening to them or help them if they needed it. God knows they'd picked one of the most dangerous places in the last century to visit. I was uncomfortable with Erimem's sudden decision to go there. There was definitely something behind that. Something had pushed her into it. That just put me more on edge.

Helena was more relaxed than me and that annoyed me. I know it was unreasonable but it did. Helena made it worse by being incredibly reasonable in return.

"You should get away from here for a few hours," she said. "Sitting watching the machine, waiting for something to happen, will drive you crazy."

"And what if they need me?"

Helena held up her phone. "We have these things, remember?"

She had a point. If I stayed I would go nuts, and I had some things at the university that needed my attention. Starting the term a fortnight late had thrown a lot of events up in the air and I needed to work on the schedule for the new Vice Chancellor. The downside of her being a friend was that she didn't mind asking for a bit extra when it came to work.

It probably made sense for me to do something constructive with the time, so I drove to the University. A couple of hours of concentrated work would be ideal for taking my mind off of whatever Erimem and Andy were doing in Stalingrad. The car park was pretty much empty with just a few cars there. Most people had the sense not to go to work on Saturday.

I had actually managed to lose myself in work for an hour when my door opened. Orla Wilton looked in. "Thought that was your Land Rover in the car park, Ibrahim."

"Catching up on a bit of work," I answered.

"Don't stay too long," Orla said. "I don't want Helena giving me an earful for overworking you."

"I won't," I promised.

"Good, now I don't feel so bad about asking another favour from you."

"Another one?" I was starting regret the politicking I did to get Orla this job. No, I wasn't. She was pushy and a pain in the arse at time but Orla was one of the most reliable and honest people I knew. After everything the University had gone through, she was exactly what we needed.

She came in and beckoned a young woman to follow her. "This is Trina Barton."

The blonde girl smiled. "Hi. How are you?" Her voice wasn't local. It was polite but she was definitely from the North East of England. Alan Shearer country. Or as my flatmate had called him, "that dirty head-kicking bastard, Shearer". I've no idea what the hatred was about but it was there, every time Match of the Day came on TV.

"Nice to meet you," I answered automatically, and looked at Orla expectantly. If I was a gambler I'd have put money on this being a friend's daughter who wanted a tour of the Egyptian exhibit. That wouldn't be too onerous.

"You have an assistant, don't you?" Orla asked.

She knew fine that I did. She had signed the papers giving final approval to Erimem being my assistant as part of her studies. "Yes," I answered. "She's... out of town this weekend."

"Nice," Orla smiled tightly. "Meet your assistant's assistant." She smiled a friendlier smile at Trina. "I'll leave you with Mr Hadmani. It's Saturday so you won't mind if you call him Ibrahim." And she was gone.

"Have a seat," I said to Trina. "I'll be back."

I caught Orla halfway down the corridor. She didn't give me a chance to speak. "Listen," she said. "You don't need another assistant but you're getting one. She's a nice girl and more importantly, her father's got more money than God and he's going to throw some of it our way. She's keen on Egyptology so you've got her for a year."

"And if I don't want her?"

Orla looked at me sourly. "Then we'll argue for a while and then I'll win. There's not a single university in the country can turn down income, Ibrahim, you know that. Even this grand old place." The annoying thing was that I couldn't disagree with her on any of that. "Make the girl useful for a year. You get an extra pair of hands for nothing, she learns something, the university pockets her dad's cash and everybody's happy. Fair enough?"

I would have argued – if I had been able to come up with a half decent argument. It was the sort of arrangement universities across the world got into regularly. The only reason I didn't want the girl around was that it would make things more complicated for myself and Erimem. We could hardly discuss the fact that I was Erimem's hundred and fifty-times great nephew with Trina about. We would have to work it out somehow. Arguing too much there and then would have made Orla suspicious, so I conceded gracefully.

"Fair enough," I said sourly.

Orla patted my arm sympathetically. "It's crap but what can we do? One thing. Don't call her a Geordie. She's from Sunderland and calling her a Geordie doesn't go well."

I went back to my office. Trina was staring out of the window. She turned as I pushed the door open.

"Sorry to get dumped on you this way," she said. "I love my

dad to bits but he can be a bit pushy sometimes. I hate it when he's flash with the cash."

That sounded like a phrase she had used before. It felt like she meant it. "No worries," I answered. "Come on. I'll show you the exhibit."

Credit where it's due. Trina obviously knew a bit about Egypt's history. She asked intelligent questions and she had respect for my country's history. More important, she had respect for the remains in the glass cases. If she hadn't... well, it wouldn't go well with Erimem. I'll never understand how she can look at the mummies of her brothers and not fall apart.

I gave Trina the half hour tour. If somebody is a pain in the backside, they get the ten minute tour. If they're a dignitary, they get an hour. Trina wasn't either of those so she got something in the middle.

I actually started to think she might be good for Erimem. We had been back for weeks and Erimem... I was going to say she didn't fit in, but how could she? She had all those memories of a different time and place with totally different customs. I was amazed she was doing as well as she was. Of course, punching a Fresher with wandering hands in the Students Union... it had taken some effort to smooth that one over. It might be good for her to spend some time with Trina – with somebody from outside of Helena, Andy and myself.

Tom Niven should have been part of that group. He had travelled to ancient Greece with us. What happened there had affected him most. He had been beaten, almost murdered and then he'd seen his girlfriend killed in front of his eyes. I'm not surprised he was struggling. I'm not surprised he stayed away from the rest of us. He'd watched me stab a man in the back. I found that hard enough to live with myself.

By the time I took Trina back to my office it was pretty much time for me to call it a day. Erimem and Andy had been gone for over three hours our time. Who knew how long that was in their time? It felt like time to go and I had done enough work to head home with a clear conscience.

I walked Trina out of the building and we agreed she would come in on Tuesday afternoon. That would give me long enough to calm Erimem down about the change in routine.

Assuming she got back from World War 2 Russia.

I was just saying goodbye to Trina when I saw Tom standing by my car.

Tom:

I'd avoided them since we got back. All of them. I didn't want to see any of them. I didn't want to see anybody. I'd thought about going back to the States, getting away from the whole damn thing. But how would I explain that? I didn't pick this University. My family sent me here. They said it would be good for me to see another country, to get some English culture in me. The shit food and crap beer... I got to like all of that. I liked some of the people and the studies didn't get in the way too much. My family has money. I could have dropped my shorts and taken a leak in the Faculty's tea-pot and they wouldn't have thrown me out. It's an Old University. It likes old money. I had three great years here. First year I went home to Boston for the Christmas Holidays. After that, I didn't bother. Mom was always busy with work and Dad? Well, who knew where the hell he was? Who cares? London was home for three years and I had fun. I loved it.

Greece took that away from me. Time travel... Romans... Greeks... it was all bullshit. It should have been fun, an adventure. They whipped me. They murdered Anna. *I murdered Anna*. It was my fault. I wanted to leave that house. I pushed her towards the door. If I'd gone first it would have been me who died. Anna died instead. I try not to think about Anna. I just can't get the image of her out of my head. What gets to me most is that I don't remember her laughing or smiling. I don't remember the fun we had in the Students Union or in bed. All I see is with a sword in her chest and blood bubbling out of her mouth. Every night when I try to sleep I see that in my head. I've tried to drink it away. I couldn't lose it in a bottle and it keeps coming back. It keeps coming back, every night. Every day. When I try to go to class. When I try to eat. When I try to sleep. It doesn't matter what I try to do. I keep seeing Anna dying.

And the thing is, I knew I deserved to feel this way. I idn't deserve any better.

I don't know why I went to see Ibrahim. I didn't want to see him. I didn't want to be reminded of anything. I just knew I couldn't go on like I was. I couldn't tell a doctor what had happened. I'd have been locked up. Except maybe Hadmani's girlfriend. I just wanted to sleep.

Ibrahim:

He looked like shit. He hadn't shaved for days. I don't think he's slept in that time either. His clothes stank of sweat and I was pretty sure he'd been crying as well. I'm not a doctor but I knew he needed one. I told him to get in the car.

Andy:

It looked like something from a horror film. Bits of uniform and skin hanging from its jaws. Erimem stood her ground. She wasn't going to show this thing she was scared. Fair enough. I was scared enough for both of us. She jabbed her sword at this thing.

"You will stop now or I will kill you."

Then the beast screeched again and that was when Erimem realised that she probably should be scared of this horrible thing in front of us. She didn't take a step back but she leaned back a few inches before squaring her shoulders again.

"You are not of this world. You will leave here and let the dead rest."

The thing screeched at us again. Bits of flesh flew from its mouth.

Erimem shouted over its howl. "You have no place here and you will not stay."

But the beast wasn't paying any attention to Erimem. It swung that sickening head in the direction of the door. A second later I could hear the sound of boots running on the concrete floor and I saw a load of soldiers running towards us. Five or six of them with their guns aimed at this demon. Their officer shouted, "Stand still!" but the creature wasn't listening. It moved like a goat on a hill, leaping up on to the pile of bodies and bounding across them before leaping up and out of a smashed window. The officer said something – I think he was swearing – and then he said the thing must have leaped over five metres to get through the window. Even in this dull light I could see that the officer was shaking. I can't say I blamed him.

Erimem was shaking as well – but she was shaking with anger. "You idiot. You frightened it away! How can I talk to it now?"

Erimem's outburst took the officer by surprise. "Calm down, Erimem," I told her. "I'm not sure that beast was going to do much talking."

"We are unlikely to find out now," she said. She sounded completely cheesed off. I got the feeling she had known the creature would be here.

That officer hadn't taken kindly to Erimem speaking to him the way she had and wanted to know who we were and what we were doing in the warehouse. He thought we were mental to have been trying to find something like that. But he wasn't daft himself. He'd had a serious shock at seeing that creature but he was ready with his questions. Why were we looking for it? Who did we work for? What did we know about it? Who were we? How the hell were we supposed to answer any of his questions? He wanted to see papers and we didn't have any. It was only when Erimem said we were looking for a clue about our friend Isabella's missing husband that the soldier paid attention. Did we know Isabella Zemanova? Were we friends of hers? That really made a difference. He introduced himself. He was Yuri Kurkov, the same Yuri Isabella had said served with her husband. His whole personality changed at that point. It was like he was with old friends and he didn't have to pretend he wasn't scared by it all. When he let his guard down you could see just how terrified he was.

Yuri left his men guarding the warehouse. Erimem said that she didn't think that the creature would come back that night. Animals that had been frightened away usually waited before coming back to their food. But Yuri left his men just in case and he led us back to Isabella's house. Somehow, knowing that creature was out there in the snow somewhere made it seem even colder.

Isabella:

I woke when I heard my door open, and I saw a man in uniform enter. In that dim light, just for a moment I thought it was Lev. But then I saw his face and recognised Yuri. And again my heart fell.

Erimem and Andy followed Yuri into the room, moving quietly so that they did not wake my boys. It surprised me that I was so relieved to see them again. Their kindness has touched me. They looked so cold. Snow was on their heads and shoulders.

"Sit," I told them. "I will make tea."

Andy replied, "Thanks. We need something to warm us up."

I put another piece of wood on the fire and waved for them to come closer to the heat. "Warm yourselves while I make tea," I said. "And then you will tell me what you find."

Andy and Erimem spoke very quietly for a few moments. Their conversation was agitated. They were disagreeing. Erimem was asking Andy to do something. Or giving her an instruction, I do not know. Andy did not like it, whatever it was. I did not ask. It was not my business. In Stalin's Russia, we knew not to ask about anything that was not our business.

Andy:

"I don't trust you," I said to Erimem. "You're going to go back out there looking for that thing on your own."

"I will not do that," Erimem answered. She looked annoyed. Good. I was pissed off and I wanted her to know it. "The beast will have returned to hiding until tomorrow night."

"So why give me this errand instead of doing it yourself?" I challenged her.

"Because I wish to learn what I can from this soldier," Erimem answered quickly. "And also..." she sighed and looked a bit embarrassed. "And also because I am not good at making the computer work." She waved her finger in the air, mimicking swiping a touchscreen. "I have tried but I cannot make it work the way you can. You will find the information quicker than I."

Actually, that made sense. She was crap with the swipe screens. Actually, she was just impatient at learning how much pressure and force to put into using them. She got annoyed when she got things wrong with them. Is it terrible that I kind of liked that I was better at something than she was? There were a lot of things I could do that she couldn't, but most of them were mundane. I was better with computers. That meant I had a purpose. I was useful. I liked how that felt.

"All right," I said, still sounding grumpy. "I'll get the information." I turned to Isabella. "Sorry, but Her Majesty is sending me on an errand. I won't be long."

I slipped out of the door without waiting for anyone to answer. I probably should have found a quiet, deserted part of the street, but there was nobody on the stairs and I didn't fancy going back out in the snow again. I grabbed the ring I wore on my middle finger and twisted it.

Ibrahim:

"Depression?" I asked Helena. "Or PTSD?"

She smiled tightly at me. "Are you just going to quote illnesses at me?" she asked. "A little knowledge is a dangerous thing."

Tom was sitting on our couch. A cup of coffee sat in front of him untouched. It had been there for the hour Helena had talked to him.

"Don't get arsey," I answered. "There's definitely something wrong with him."

"There is," Helena nodded her head in agreement. "But I

don't think it's bipolar or PTSD. He has some of the symptoms and he's probably borderline but I think he's just coping with the guilt. In my medical opinion I'd say he doesn't need medicated, other than to get him a good night's sleep. He does need to talk about it, though."

"Did he talk about what happened?" I asked. Helena had made me leave the room.

"A little," she said. "I probably shouldn't tell you any of this. Patient-doctor confidentiality and that kind of thing… I'm not sure it applies here, though."

"So what do we do?" I asked.

"You're still having nightmares about Greece," Helena said, squeezing my arm. "Talk to him about that. Let him know he's not the only one struggling to deal with it. He needs to know he's not alone." She nodded towards the kitchen. "I'll be making fresh coffee. Decaf, naturally." She paused thoughtfully. "He should sleep in the spare room tonight. He can have a couple of the sleeping pills you had when you were recovering."

"Fair enough." Helena went to make coffee and I sat on the couch beside Tom. Not too close that I'd spook him but close enough that he didn't feel that I was putting distance between us. "Don't blame you for not touching the coffee," I said. "I make terrible coffee."

"This is England. Everybody makes terrible coffee."

"One day I'll get you some traditional Egyptian coffee," I told him. "That will clear your sinuses."

He didn't smile. He flexed his mouth like he was trying to but it didn't happen.

Small talk wasn't going to get us anywhere. It was best just to say what I needed to. "I still dream about it," I said. "I still ache from the gunshot but painkillers deal with that. The memories…" I sucked in a deep breath. "They're harder to get rid of." Tom didn't answer but I knew he was listening. I carried on. "It's nearly every night. I remember it. Being shot, lying there in that room thinking I was going to die." Just talking about it brought everything back. "I remember stabbing the Vice Chancellor in the back." I could remember every part of it... the panic when I thought he was going to kill Erimem and Andy, the resistance as the tip of by sword touched his skin. I even remembered how it felt as the blade hit bones as it went through him. "I don't remember the moment I decided to do it," I said quietly. "Maybe because I don't want to remember when I decided to kill another human being."

"He's have killed the other two," Tom said. I sounded like he was saying what he thought he was expected to say.

"He would have," I agreed. "He'd have killed them and then he'd have killed us. I know it was the only option I had, but... it doesn't change that I did it." I picked up Tom's cold coffee and took a sip. I didn't want to drink it, I just wanted a moment to pull my thoughts together. "I didn't want to kill anyone. He gave me no choice. It wasn't my fault. It wasn't any of our fault. The Vice Chancellor and his friends put in that position. They're to blame not us. That doesn't make it any easier, though."

"No, it doesn't."

"I still dream about it most nights," I continued. "But a few weeks ago it was every night. Now it's not. I've been lucky. I was able to talk with Helena about it. With Erimem and Andy as well, but mostly Helena." His eyes glanced up at me and I locked mine on them. "You have to talk about it. It's like a boil that needs to burst so you can let the poison out. If that sounds sage in any way... I stole it from Helena."

"We don't talk," Tom mumbled. "In my family. Mom always taught us, if you have a problem, don't talk about it. It makes you weak." He shrugged. "If we ever had a problem, she wasn't interested. Unless it was bad for business or the family reputation."

I could recognise the attitude. I'd seen it with school friends. I didn't like it any more than I had when I was a kid, "I'm not your mother," I said. "I haven't got the hips for it, for one thing. For another, if you want to talk, I'll listen. I'm pretty sure Helena will as well."

He didn't answer but he did nod. That was probably the most grateful nod I'd ever seen in my life.

Helena had just brought the coffee in and put a fresh mug in from of Tom when the door opened again and Andy bundled in. She was wearing her winter coat and she looked freezing.

Andy:

I didn't expect to see Tom Niven when I went back into Ibrahim's flat. I definitely didn't expect to see him in that state. Christ, he was a mess. Ibrahim looked ashen as well. Whatever they'd been talking about I probably hadn't helped by barging in. Who am I kidding? It didn't take a rocket scientist to work out what they'd been talking about. They'd been hurt worst by Greece. Maybe they would deal with it better together. When I saw Helena was there I didn't feel quite so bad about barging in.

"You're back," Helena said. She sounded relieved then she wrinkled her face. "Or course you're back. You're standing there. You're both all right?"

"Well, yeah..." I said uncertainly. I moved aside so they could see Erimem wasn't with me. "Erimem sent me back," I explained. "She wanted me to check the computer in the..." I stopped. Tom didn't know that the stone chamber where we'd seen some really awful things happen had been transformed into a pretty snazzy villa. He didn't know we'd moved the portal to it either. Maybe that was something he'd be better off not knowing. "She wanted me to check something on the computer in her room."

"Ah, right." Helena could see what I meant. So could Ibrahim.

"I'll go and get on with it." I hurried back to the ordinary looking door on the hall's wall and stepped through into Erimem's villa.

The cult who had captured the Habitat had discovered a huge database but they had only used it to track Erimem. They hadn't really investigated it at all. I wanted to but I didn't really dive into it like I should. It just didn't feel right. This Habitat was stolen. The information wasn't really ours to take. No, that was crap. I was scared, that was the truth. I was scared of what I would find in that machine. The weird thing is, I'm not sure why I was scared of it. I'm curious by nature. I've always hoovered in information. I wanted to go to Uni... I was even accepted to Uni before Dad walked out. I wanted to learn, I wanted to find out new things. This just felt wrong, like maybe it was stuff we shouldn't know. Stuff we weren't ready to know. Maybe that's crap I picked up from a sci-fi movie. I don't know. Whatever it was, it had stopped me really looking into the huge banks of information. I didn't have a choice now, though. Erimem had given me a job to do. I swiped my finger across one of the panels and starting keying in the information I wanted the machine to search for. I would take time to find what I wanted and I wondered if I had time to run to the local supermarket.

Ibrahim:

We put Tom into the spare room and Helena handed him a couple of sleeping pills to take. I know she didn't like them.

She had a bee in her bonnet about the way some doctors over-prescribed them to patients. I thought that was a thing of the past. She wasn't having any of that. In this case she made an exception. Mine too. Sometimes a patient just needs rest. When we were sure Tom was asleep we went through into Erimem's villa. It was late at night by then but it was still day in that artificial little world. I got the feeling that could play havoc with a person's body clock. Andy would have to regulate that better.

We found Andy scribbling furiously in a notebook, copying notes from one of the screens. There were pictures of God only knows what on the screen. It was sort of the shape of a man but obviously it wasn't human. The joints were wrong, the angles of the body too. That horrible leathery skin and bony head. Even in a picture those rows of teeth were terrifying.

"What is that thing?" I asked Andy. "And why does Erimem need to know about it?"

Andy:

I told Ibrahim what had happened in Stalingrad. He wanted to yank Erimem straight back from there on the spot. That wasn't going to happen. He didn't know how to do it and I didn't want Erimem pissed off at me. I understood why Ibrahim was worried. Of course I did. I'd seen that thing. I saw what it was eating. I didn't want to meet that damn thing again, so I understood Ibrahim. And I didn't understand what Erimem was doing with this whole Stalingrad thing, but I did trust her. She was my friend. She had saved my life and she'd made me laugh. I trusted her. Besides, from what I'd discovered about that alien, it had no place on Earth back on 1942 or at any time. So I was scared of what was happening back there and uncomfortable that she wasn't telling me everything but I trusted her.

I held up my notes. "I should take these to Erimem," I said. "She needs to know what I've found out."

Ibrahim didn't like that. He didn't like it a bit. He called me a bloody idiot. When he accepted he wasn't going to change my mind about going back he grumbled that he was going to have to go back with me. Helena wasn't having any of that. She just wasn't letting that happen. Ibrahim wasn't going to back down either. They both had a point but they were wasting time. I've got to admit it was a bit uncomfortable watching them have a domestic. It wasn't exactly like watching your parents argue but it felt weird. Maybe it was because it was the first time I'd seen them disagreeing.

I started zipping up my coat. "Look, I need to get back to Stalingrad."

Helena scowled at me. "It's time travel. You don't have to worry about a few minutes one way or the other." She turned her glare to Ibrahim. "You almost died last time. Not again."

Ibrahim sounded exasperated. "Do you think I should let her go back there on her own?"

"Back where?"

We hadn't noticed Tom come into the room.

Ibrahim:

We had assumed Tom would be asleep. He was exhausted. We had left him with a couple of sleeping tablets. He had been looking for water to wash the tablets down. We had been careless. We left the door to Erimem's villa open, so when he got up…

Shit. Stupid of us.

It didn't take him long to work out the basics of what had happened, especially when he saw that five sided control table. It had been made of stone the last time he saw it. Even though it was all swipe screens and shining black edging there was no doubt it was the same thing. You could see it in his face when he realised what this place actually was. You could actually see it sinking in to him as he looked around.

"We reprogrammed it," Andy eventually explained. Tom just nodded. He moved back out into the living room of the villa. He touched the leather couch and the wooden table that sat between the two couches that faced each other. I wondered if he thought he had actually gone mad.

"Come on," I said to Tom. "I'll get you some water to wash down those pills."

"No. Do you have a heavy coat I can borrow?" He nodded at Andy. "I'm going with her."

Tom:

I didn't do it for Andy or for Erimem.

Saying I would go with her to wherever she was going... it wasn't for them.

It was for me.

They had gone somewhere dangerous and Andy was going back. I'd spent weeks feeling guilty and helpless. Anna had died and I hadn't done anything to stop it. Maybe if I went with Andy I could be useful, keep an eye on her and Erimem. I didn't want to be a hero or anything like that. I just needed to stop feeling guilty.

Andy:

The trip back to Stalingrad dumped Tom and me in more or less the same place Erimem and I arrived the first time we landed. It was every bit as cold this time around.

"This way," I said to him. He pulled Ibrahim's coat tighter around himself and followed me. He didn't talk. Neither did I. I didn't like him. Who am I kidding? I'd hated him for a long time. He had spent years at the Uni being the rich kid who let everybody know how rich he was. He screwed his way through God knows how many women and told everybody who he'd got into his bed. And if they said no, he lied and said he'd screwed them anyway. He'd done that with Sasha. She was a student at the Uni, We were... what we were was nobody's business but ours. He lied and said he'd screwed her. Truth was she had turned him down flat. But after he told his stories, everybody thought she was another of his conquests and she hated that. She hated being thought of that way. She was from Ukraine, right on the border with Moldova. She said opinions of people matter there. A lot of the society is about putting on a show. Things like having a big house. Didn't matter if you couldn't afford to heat it, as long as you had the big house. Big house, good job, good reputation so her mum could say her daughter was better than the others in her town. It sounded like shit to me but it mattered to Sasha. When she started getting the hassle because that prick Niven had lied... well, she's studying in Edinburgh now. The time between emails and Skype chats is growing all the time. He crapped on our lives because he couldn't deal with being told a woman wasn't interested. I hated him for that.

I could see he was struggling and I felt like a complete bitch for still feeling that hate for him nagging at my head. I focused on finding the way back to Isabella's house. It proved easy enough. My sense of direction is pretty good. Okay, so is the old street-map of Stalingrad I printed from the internet.

We got to the house and were hurrying up the stairs when I saw a flash of electricity on a landing. I hurried up. I wondered if Erimem had decided to go back to 2015. Maybe I'd been gone too long? I pushed open the door and went inside. Erimem glanced up. "Do you need something before you go?" she asked.

"What do you mean?"

She looked back, clearly a bit bemused. "You left only a few moments ago." She peered at my shoulders and head. "How did you come to be so covered in snow?"

"Because we just walked in it for half an hour." I stepped aside and pulled Tom into the flat, closing the door behind him. "You're letting the heat out."

Seeing Tom took Erimem by surprise. She usually hid something like that pretty well but this caught her out. "I did not expect to see you," she said.

Tom shrugged, spilling snow from his shoulders on to the floor. "Didn't expect to be here," he admitted.

Erimem had already moved on from being surprised about Tom. "You have clearly been gone for some time. How long would you say you were away from here?"

I checked my watch. "About four hours altogether."

She sucked her bottom lip thoughtfully. "And yet to us you were gone a minute at most." She held up her thumb and indicated the ornate time travel ring. "It seems these are not as precise as we would have hoped."

I had to agree. "Looks that way. Still, they got us here, more or less."

"Did you find anything in the computer?" she asked.

I pulled my notes from inside my jacket and handed them over. "Plenty, and none of it makes good reading."

Erimem started reading. Isabella was looking at Tom and me, totally confused. She didn't understand how I could suddenly be so cold and covered in snow when I hadn't even had time to get down the stairs to the building's front door. She can't have had a clue about Tom either.

"You are cold. You need tea."

Isabella:

It did not make sense. This girl, Andy... how did she have time to be covered in snow? I could see it was thick on her boots like she had walked many kilometres. I did not understand, but since the war began there were many things I did not understand. It was not a real time. I say that badly. It was a time that did not feel real, like the rules of our real world had been taken away for a time. In the real world, a country would not bomb civilians from another country for no reason. In the real world, a country could not be run by a madman like Hitler. And yet in the real world, my country was ruled by a madman like Stalin. Madmen like Hitler and Stalin had taken away our real lives. They had destroyed our lives and taken so much from us. All the dead, all those who still breathed but carried the stain of death in them. I think the boy who had come back with Andy had seen death. He had the same look in his eyes I saw in many young soldiers. There was nothing I could do for them except offer them tea.

Tom:

I've never liked tea. The British are obsessed with it. Maybe because they're so shit at making coffee. This wasn't like the tea back in London. I'd never actually enjoyed tea before. It was weak but it was hot, and I sat and hugged my cup while

Erimem told us what she had picked up from the notes Andy brought back.

"The creature we saw tonight was a Drofen, one of a species called the Drofen Horde. They travel the..." she paused, looking at Isabella and the soldier who had been introduced as Yuri. "Well, they travel looking for worlds filled with the dying."

"Worlds?" Isabella shook her head in confusion. "You mean that they travel the world."

"No," Erimem said. "I mean that they travel through the universe looking for worlds filled with the dead. They are carrion feeders, as hyenas and eagles often are at home. They feed on the dead."

Isabella wasn't buying it. Maybe she just didn't want to believe it. "It is not possible!"

"Perhaps," Erimem agreed. "But ask Yuri if what he saw tonight was possible."

Isabella looked at Yuri and he couldn't look her in the eye. You could tell he didn't want to admit that Erimem was right, not even to himself. Aye, but he knew well enough. He knew that what he'd seen had no business on Earth. "Where does it come from?" he asked Erimem.

Isabella:

Yuri is not a fool or a coward. He is a brave soldier who faced death many times every day. If he had denied Erimem's words of this creature being of another world, I would have believed him. Other worlds, they are the stories of small boys, of writers like Verne and Wells. Lev had read their books to me – I do not know if they were legal in our country – but I had laughed. I found them foolish and fanciful. Now I asked my new friend, "Is this a war between different worlds, Erimem?"

Andy:

"No, my friend," Erimem told her. "The Drofen are fearsome creatures but they have not been warriors for thousands of years. They prefer dead flesh now."

But there was something in Erimem's voice. She wasn't telling us everything, I was sure she was hiding something. I had only skimmed the pages as I printed them, So I asked her, "Yeah, and the rest."

She bit on her lip and glanced at me before she answered. "There are stories… just rumours, as far as Andy could find in the computer, but it is possible that some of the Drofen still prefer live meat."

"And you went to face one on your own?" I said to her. "You're completely nuts."

"I did not know exactly what they were when I came here," Erimem admitted. "But at least now we do know more about these creatures because I went in search of the creature."

Yuri asked where these Drofen came from. Erimem rattled off the name of a planet and a star so fast none of us caught them, but Yuri believed Erimem. So did Isabella. You could see it in their faces. It was a look I think I probably wore at some time in Greece. The look of people suddenly having to believe in the impossible. Yuri asked how long it had been in Stalingrad.

There was no way Erimem could know that but she was fairly sure that it wouldn't be alone. "They move in groups, you see. Their society has a very rigid structure. Actually it is quite like that of wolves."

Then she stopped talking. She was looking at Isabella.

Isabella:

I did not cry. I had no tears left. I had shed them all in the weeks before then. But Erimem saw in my face what I was thinking. They were talking of these creatures – these were the creatures who had probably taken my husband. When they talked of what these Drofen did… it was what they must have done to Lev. I would not be weak. Germany would not make me weak. I would not let these Drofen do this either.

"How can they be stopped?" I asked.

I listened as Erimem and Andy spoke. Normally the Drofen stayed only as long as the war lasted. They would scavenge the dead. When there was nothing left for them, they moved on. But there was so much for them in Stalingrad. They would have to be forced to leave. They did not say how but under Erimem's kindness there was steel and I saw that this young woman was never a person I would want as an enemy.

She said, "I am going to talk with their leader. They are an intelligent race. I hope they will listen to reason."

"You are insane," I told her. "They will kill you."

When she smiled, there was a look of real cunning in Erimem's eyes. "Not if I am already dead."

Andy:

Erimem's plan was so simple it didn't even deserve the name. She was going to play dead and wait for one of these Drofen things to take her to its spaceship. She was sure it was somewhere in the city, hidden by a camouflage shield.

I told her straight. "Play dead? You'll wind up dead and then where will you be?"

She wouldn't be talked out of it. God, she's a stubborn cow when she's got her mind set on doing something.

But I could be just as much of a stubborn cow as she could. "I'm coming with you," I said. Oh, she tried to argue but I was having none of it. I wouldn't interfere unless I thought this creature was liable to take a bite out of her but I'd be there all the same.

We spent the morning working out the places where the Drofen had been seen and worked out the territory they were most likely to be in and used that to work out the best place for Erimem to stake herself out.

I genuinely hated her plan.

Isabella:

Morning did not bring any break from the cold. Only more snow. More snow and more German shells and bombs, closer to the house than before. It would not be long before this house was also broken and good only for people to salvage wood for their fires from the wreckage. I did not know where I would go when that happened.

I fed my boys with food brought by my new friends and hugged them, but I did it without thinking. In my mind I thought only of Lev. I wondered if he was dead, if they had… I could not bear to think the word. If they had *eaten* him. I had accepted the thought that he might be killed. He was a soldier. That he might die is something that every soldier and his family must accept. That he might be eaten… not a person anymore, just meat… I could not bear this.

We went out twice in the day. The first time was to scavenge wood from any houses that had been hit by German fire. While we did this, Yuri returned to his duty. The second trip was not so good. All of the wood that could be taken was already gone. I knew it would be like this, but I could not sit in my house and do nothing. I spoke with people who might have seen Lev. None of them had. But some had seen the demon. Most made blessings on themselves when they talked of this beast.

I was not accurate about one thing I said here. When we went out those times it was only Andy and the boy, Tom, who were with me. Erimem went with Yuri when he went to his barracks. They had much to discuss about her plan. I did not like her idea she and Yuri had created and said this to her when she came back. Andy agreed with me. Erimem did not reply. Instead she made funny faces for the children. She knew she could not help everyone. I think this Erimem had much sadness in her. Much sadness.

Erimem:

When I discussed battle tactics and strategies it was always with my dear friend, Antranak, never with my father. I was a daughter who was never to be Pharaoh, and so he would never have thought of teaching me battle tactics. After my brothers were killed, he realised that I needed to be taught, but his heart was so full of despair and sorrow he could not give the task the effort it required. But still I had an excellent teacher. Antranak was a great soldier and a fearsome warrior. I saw him in battle many times. It was as if he became younger when he was in battle. Years dropped from him. He was as good a teacher as he was a warrior. One thing he told me often so that I would never forget was that knowledge was as powerful a weapon as a sword.

"Know your enemy's strengths and weaknesses," he told

me. "Turn their weaknesses into your strengths. It will save the lives of your troops and possibly yourself."

I listened to Antranak and always kept that guidance in my mind: knowledge is a weapon.

I have always found the hours before a battle very difficult if I do not occupy myself. Normally I would have discussed tactics or spent time with my generals but in this case I had no generals and my tactics were very simple. So, I was left with dull hours ahead of me in which I could only become tense.

I asked Yuri if it would be possible for me to join him when he returned to his duties. He thought me mad for my request but I persuaded him by saying that I needed to see more of the land to be better prepared for this night ahead. He agreed and allowed me to accompany him to his barracks. It was a dismal place in the basement of what had once been a great building. Most of the upper floors were now gone. Chunks of them lay scattered across the ground we crossed to a set of stone steps which led down to a battered old door.it was not the original door for this building. I could see it did not fit properly. The inside of the frame had been widened to stop the worst of the wind getting through. It was not completely successful.

Yuri's men were waiting for him. They were exhausted. I could see it in their faces and in how they stood. They were hungry and they had been pushed beyond the pointed any person should be pushed. Only soldiers ever have the look of these men. Only soldiers who have seen too much and given too much.

The soldiers showed no surprise or interest on hearing that I was joining them on patrol. One of them simply shrugged and stated that it was not his job to ask questions.

The snow lightened as we set out from the barracks. There had been fires burning in the troops' base but it had still felt cold. That made the cold hit me harder when I went outside again. It also felt as if the lighter snow had brought a further drop in temperature. I pulled my coat tighter around me and thought for a moment of Egypt's sun.

Yuri broke my dream. He nudged me and handed me a black pistol. He said it was a Tokarev and it had belonged to an officer who was killed a few days earlier. It did not feel as natural in my hand as a sword but it had good balance and I was comfortable with it there. I thanked him and pushed it into a pocket.

We walked for thirty minutes moving closer to the sounds of explosions and gunfire. The damage to the buildings grew worse with every street that took us away from the centre of the city. Nobody could live in this place now. It felt like a dead city.

The soldiers stayed close to the walls, ready to find what protection they could if it was needed. They did not speak except to say it was safe to move or if they saw something suspicious. They did not have the strength for anything else.

I stayed close to the walls, also. I looked at the wreckage ahead and to the side of us. There were so many places for an enemy to wait in ambush. The soldiers were looking to the same places I was. They were experienced, probably more experienced than I was.

The attack came suddenly and swiftly. The stone walls beside our heads began to spit chips as bullets slammed against them. Two of the soldiers ahead of me dropped. One had been shot in the stomach, the other in the face. Both would be dead before long. I could not think of them. Dealing with our enemy or finding cover was what mattered. Yuri pushed his men through into a broken building shouting that the walls would give us cover. I pulled myself through a shattered window and dropped on to a floor of snow. The others pushed through a doorway. One took a bullet to his leg as he tried to shut the door.

"Piotr?" Yuri asked of me. "And Yusef?"

"We cannot help them," I answered. "We must save ourselves."

The enemies – sometimes called Nazis, sometimes called Germans – I do not understand the difference, broke from cover behind a shattered building fifty paces ahead of us and charged. They knew we had lost men and they outnumbered us. They looked desperate, wrapped in layers of clothes that flapped in the wind. Yuri told his men to wait, to hold their fire until the enemy men were hardly fifteen paces away. Their aim was good and from behind the wall they killed five of the enemy without taking more injuries themselves, but then these Germans were on us. They had long daggers on the end of their guns and used them as spears to stab at us. One of Yuri's men tried to block the door, but the Germans used windows. They could not be stopped as a group and it quickly became individual battles between one of them and one of us. Large battles always break into individual confrontations like that. I saw a Russian speared in the stomach with that dagger on the gun a moment before the gun cracked loudly and a bullet followed the dagger into my comrade's stomach. I did not think. I pulled the *gladius* I carried and swung it down across the German's arm. I felt it slash through cloth, flesh and muscle till it hit bone. He screamed until the handle of the sword smashed into his face and silenced him. I drove the sword hard into his chest and pulled it free as his knees buckled.

The numbers of our forces were even and these Germans fought desperately. I stabbed and cut at several of their men until I saw one of them aim his rifle at me. I was too far from him to attack and there was nowhere for me to hide. I accepted that I would die. The German's head jerked backwards, a spray of red showering the snow as the side of his skull disappeared. Yuri did not wait for my thanks. He turned back to the German he fought. I owed Yuri a debt and repaid it by slashing the *gladius* hard along the back of his opponent's neck.

The battle finished quickly after that. We had more men and their remaining soldiers had no way to escape. None were taken prisoner. The Russians killed them. One was tormented before being put out of his misery at the end of his own dagger – a bayonet, Yuri called it. They gutted him and then stripped these Germans of everything they had. Clothes, weapons, equipment... everything was taken. I looked at the blood staining the snow around them. My comrades had found that their enemies had nothing worth stealing. Their clothing was thin and worthless against this cold, their ammunition was meagre and they carried no food. Their scrawny bodies told me they had not been fed properly for a long time.

At the place from which the Germans had launched their first attack we found a pile of wood. They had been scavenging in the city for a way to stay warm. This was a poorly equipped and badly supplied army. Their only hope was that the Russians were equally short on supplies. This was a bad war. Neither side was prepared for it. Good men would die because their superiors had failed. I was not surprised the Drofen had chosen this place. Stalingrad was a feast for them.

We collected our fallen and carried them back to the barracks. We left the Germans to the snow – or to the Drofen.

Iain McLaughlin

PART THREE

Iain McLaughlin

Andy:

The bombs were getting closer to Isabella's house. We heard a house collapse just a few streets away early in the afternoon. Isabella pretended that she hadn't noticed it. What kind of life is it when you're pretending you don't notice something like that?

A bomb had flattened a factory in the heart of the territory the Drofen had been spotted in most often. We made our way there just before the sun went down. Not that you could actually see the sun through the cloud. As we left, just outside her house, Isabella gave Erimem a huge hug. Not me or Tom, you understand, just her. Yuri held out a pistol to Erimem and she slipped it into a pocket inside her coat. She had her sword as well. I was relieved she wasn't going into this unarmed but I had my doubts that whatever she carried would be enough. I couldn't shake the image of that thing tearing at flesh and bone with those teeth.

Isabella stayed behind in her flat with her kids. The rest of us went with Erimem. If anything it was colder than ever. Freezing wind blowing in wave after wave of large flakes. We were white by the time we got to the end of the street.

The factory was a real mess. The roof was completely gone and so was the majority of one of the walls. It had been on two floors. Most of what had been upstairs had collapsed through to the ground level. Yuri said that nobody had been killed because the bomb had hit before the workers had arrived, so there wouldn't be any other bodies around to distract the Drofen.

"That's all fine and well," I said. "But what if this Drofen thing decides to take a bite out of Erimem while she's pretending to be dead?"

She pulled her coat tighter around herself. "Then I shall do my very best to give it indigestion."

She probably thought that was really funny. I didn't. I could have punched her.

Erimem settled herself down in a fairly open bit of ground. After a moment she hauled a toppled table a bit closer to protect herself from the wind. Honestly. She was offering herself as some kind of monster's dinner but she was more worried about catching a cold. I settled into a protected little bit of shelter that gave me a good look at Erimem but gave me plenty of cover. The jacket was keeping me warm enough and I'd picked up a second woolly hat when I went back to the twenty first century. Tom was in a similar kind of fox hole as me and Yuri headed away to take up a position on what was left of the first floor along with some of his soldiers. The same ones who'd been at the warehouse. You could tell they didn't want to be there. In the distance we could hear gunfire and shelling. The soldiers would have been more at home dealing with that that with what they'd seen at the factory.

I tried to relax and get comfortable. I couldn't understand for the life of me how Erimem could just lie there in the freezing cold without shivering. She wasn't moving at all. In fact nothing was moving. It was like that for hours, just that eerie night-time glow from the snow and the sound of wind and big guns in the distance. It was much too cold to get any sleep but I did close my eyes – just for a minute you understand – to rest my eyes from the snow. Then I heard a sound. There was movement in the rubble. I looked out and there was that terrible thing, not six feet from my hideout. It had its back to me but I could see the wet leathery skin and the curve of that bony head. I didn't dare breathe as it looked around, and then it moved away towards Erimem. It's hard to explain exactly how it moved. In some ways it was like a frog the way its legs bent but it had something like a lizard about it as well, the way its legs swung out when it ran. Jesus, it could move fast. Really fast. It took no time at all for it to be beside Erimem. I hoped Yuri and his soldiers were ready to fire if it decided to try eating Erimem. But instead it just picked her up and threw her across its shoulder like she weighed nothing at all. And then it was moving away, leaping and running through the snow and ice carrying her like she was a kid.

The plan had been that we would follow, but not too closely. That wasn't a problem. The Drofen moved so fast we could hardly keep it in sight. I was a good bit ahead of Yuri and his men but it wasn't long before I was having to guess which way this Drofen thing was going. And I wondered if I'd lost her for good.

Isabella:

Erimem told me that she was awake all the time she was being carried by this demon. She had forced herself to relax all of the muscles in her body. She had been awake but she had made no noise and no movement. She did not dare move – or even open her eyes – until she knew she was inside some kind of ship and she heard a door close. Even then she waited some minutes before opening her eyes. She was in a great room, filled with dead soldiers and civilians. Many dozens of them. She could not count all of them. There were too many. She called it a larder. She would not tell me everything that she saw there. She thinks it is her duty to protect people.

She opened the door of her chamber with the sword she carried. The locks on the doors were unlike anything I had seen but she said they were weak. She thought it was because they did not expect their food to try to escape. When she left that room of the dead, Erimem was in a corridor, metal and narrow. The metal was dull like it was dirty, covered with a film of old

oil. The ship smelled of rotting flesh. It smelled like death.
There were other doors and she opened them in turn and
explored. Behind one of the doors she found people living,
huddled together in fear, afraid that these monsters had come
for them. They screamed and cried out until they realised that
Erimem was only a human being like them.

And I also stopped screaming.

She was shocked to see me there. She was furious and
demanded to know how I came to be in that place.

I explained to her. I did not think I should need to defend
my actions to her. I know I sounded angry. "Lev is my
husband. I do not know if you can find him. When you left
today... I was frustrated. I wanted to help find my Lev but I did
not know how. So I went to look as I have done often. I looked
in many places he has visited before one of these things –
Drofen you call them – found me, cornered me in a broken
house. It caught me and carried me here." For a moment she
was very angry and asked how I could be so stupid but her
anger faded quickly and the concerned look returned to her
face.

"I must get you away from here," she said. "You are not
going to die here." She led me to the door and others followed.
She pointed along the corridor. "The hatch leading out into the
city is back that way," she told me.

"But what about you?" I asked. "You do not come with
us?"

She answered, "No. No, I must go and face the leader of
these Drofen."

She was crazy and I told her this but she would not hear me.
She told us to go. But I am stubborn also. I would not leave.
"Lev is my husband. I will not leave until I know what
happened to him. I will stay with you." And now she called me
a crazy woman. "Then we are crazy together, Erimem," I said.

She did not have time to argue. The other prisoners

followed directions Erimem gave and I followed her as she hurried in the opposite direction along these vile metal corridors with their oily walls. I think it was less than a minute when we saw one of the creatures ahead of us. I gripped Erimem's hand It was a reflex, not something I realised I did until I felt her squeeze my hand. She breathed very deeply and then walked towards the beast.

"You," she said very clearly. "Yes, you. I want to talk to you." She took a small step backwards and almost knocked me over as this thing turned to us and looked at us with black, dead eyes. In this light I could see that its face was something between a bird and a lizard. It was like something spat out of hell. And then it was like Erimem had remembered she should be brave and she pulled himself up so she looked taller. "I am a Queen, a leader of armies. I am not accustomed to being forced to wait by underlings." She smiled at me. A sweet, innocent smile and said, "I do not lie, Isabella. In my own land I was once Queen.". I did not doubt her. She turned back to this Drofen creature and said, "You will take me to your leader now."

Tom:

We had lost her. We'd been given one simple job to do and somewhere in the snow and rubble we'd screwed it up. I could feel that guilt coming back. I was going to let somebody else die because I wasn't able to protect them like I should. Yuri wasn't so desperate about it. He thought there was only one place in this direction they could be hiding. But when we got here there was nothing. Just broken buildings and more snow and ice. Then there was a dull sort of light. It didn't come from anywhere. It just floated about five feet off the ground, a tiny spot of light. Then it widened out into a circle about six feet high and we could see the inside of what looked like a spaceship floating there, up in the air. We could see there were people inside it, looking terrified.

"Come on," It was Andy who said that. It should have been me. "It's just camouflaged. We need to get the people away from there."

They were frightened but Yuri's boys were as brave as anyone I can imagine. How brave do they have to be to be so scared but to do what they need to anyway? When they saw their people in that light, they just ran to help. We got them away as quick as we could but they moved so slowly. One of them said that a dark skinned girl had set them free. That had to be Erimem. And they also said that Erimem had a woman named Isabella with her. I asked which way Erimem had gone in the ship. Yuri shouted at me to stop but I was in the ship and on my way before he finished.

Isabella:

It took us deeper into the ship, this awful thing. We passed more of its kind. Some became guards around us. Erimem refused to show fear to any of them. Their breath stank. Everything about them stank. Even in this cold I could smell raw meat and rotting meat. I was terrified and stayed close to Erimem. I noticed that she kept her hand close to the front of her coat so she could grip the sword she carried. She should have kept the gun but she had forced it into my hands. "If we must fight, you will fight," she had told me. If we had to fight, I did not think we would win. I looked in every door and passage we passed but I saw nothing. The stink was foul. All of it was the smell of rotting meat. Rotting people. I tasted bile in my throat.

The leader's room was large and its walls were the same oily metal as all the others. But it had grandness. On the walls there were moving images of a strange place. Wet land with plants I did not recognise and a pink and red sky. There were deep pools of water in the floor.

The leader was stretched out, resting by a panel which glowed with heat. It snarled with anger when we were brought in. It opened its mouth and I could hear a voice. It spoke in Russian. My language. The words seemed wrong coming from that mouth. They did not belong there. I did not know how but the ring Erimem had handed to me earlier, the ring that had made me feel that it was burning my flesh when I put it on my finger, I knew it had something to do with this.

The leader of these Drofen asked why we had been brought there. Erimem did not let our Drofen guards answer. She said, "Listen to me. I name you as the Drofen Horde, children of Monoceretos, and I demand that you cease your actions on this planet."

It could not believe her words. "You demand?" It rose on to its hind legs. They bent differently than ours do. This one was different even than those around us. It was bigger, it looked stronger. Definitely it was more frightening.

"Yes, I demand," Erimem answered. But she did not sound so confident when the creature moved closer. There was a small shake in her voice, Small but I noticed it. "You are the leader here?" she asked.

The creature said that it was the Horde Prime. Erimem nodded as if she recognised this title. It think it was not true, a bluff. "Then you are the one I have come to talk with. You have been scavenging the dead of this terrible conflict."

It said, "They are meat."

"Only when they are dead," Erimem answered sharply. "By your laws and by galactic treaty to which you have signed your agreement, you are only allowed to scavenge the dead."

This monster said that it knew the laws. And then Erimem asked, did its people know the laws?

It looked at her but did not answer. Erimem went on and her voice was strong. She had passion in her words. "Do you know that your people are taking living humans? In a city filled with thousands of dead, your people are killing dozens, possibly hundreds more."

And the creature said this terrible thing again. "They are meat."

"So you do know what is going on here." In this moment, Erimem sounded both sad and angry. "I had hoped that you did not."

It said, "Nothing happens on my ship that I do not know."

"As it should be," Erimem said. "A leader should know everything that happens under their command." She paused. "A leader must also accept the guilt and bear the consequences of those actions." She let the sentence stand as a threat before continuing. "But I will allow you to leave this planet unharmed if you leave now and return all the humans you have on your ship – the living and the dead."

A terrible sound came from the creature. I do not know if it was amused or angry. I know only that this sound truly belonged to a demon from hell. "We will feast on this world," it said. "The dead and the living. Fresh meat, living meat as we ate in the times when we hunted our prey and ate the flesh as it kicked its last. Before we became weak."

Erimem looked at this fearsome creature and she was not afraid. I believe in my soul she was not afraid even though this beast was far larger and more powerful than she. "For the last time, leave this world," she said.

"No."

"Then I have no choice," Erimem said. And from her pocket she pulled a radio set. Something like a walkie-talkie, I think they are called. "I do not think you see absolutely everything that happens on your ship," she said. "If you did, you would have seen that I carry this and when I speaking into it…" She pressed a button and spoke into it. "Now, Yuri." She threw the radio aside. "What happens now is your responsibility." A second later, an explosion shook this place. And then more, one after the other. The creature ran to look at machines around his walls. "Your cloak is destroyed and your engines are crippled," Erimem said. Another explosion shook us. It was bigger and shook us harder. "The first explosions were grenades. These will be Yuri's mortars opening fire. Your ship is visible and taking damage." Another explosion made me stagger.

It turned to us, a monster that did not belong in this world and I did believe in demons and hell. I knew that it would kill us. But it would be stopped and that was more important. Erimem pulled me behind her and she drew her sword. "Even if you kill me there is no escape for you." The creature did not care. It screamed in rage and flew towards us. Erimem thrust her sword forward to stab at the beast… but then it was send backwards by an explosion behind me. A great hole appeared in its chest. Yuri stood behind us, a rifle in his hand.

Andy:

Yuri didn't have time to think. Probably for the best. He just lifted his gun and shot the beast. Before it could stand he shot it again. In the head, this time. Brains and skull splattered on the metal deck. Yuri would have kept shooting until he had no ammunition left, I'm sure of that, but Erimem caught his arm. We didn't have long before the German army started shelling. If everything was going to plan, Yuri's lads had fired a load of their mortars out at the Germans to get their interest.

The Germans would reply by retaliating in force with heavy artillery, hopefully destroying the spaceship. Another explosion blasted into the side of the ship and the corridor behind us collapsed, all twisted metal and fire. The whole ship shook and Isabella stumbled towards me, almost knocking me off my feet. I heard a horrible sound of tearing metal above me. I started to move but a hand grabbed me and pulled me in the other direction. Isabella was hauled with me. A broad metal panel with some kind of support girder slammed down where we would have been running to. Tom had pulled us back from that. If he hadn't, we'd have been dead. How do you thank somebody for that? What do you say? Especially to somebody you've hated so much. 'Thank you' wouldn't have been enough. It didn't matter. He was as uncomfortable as me and he turned away to look at Erimem. She looked at the blocked doorway and then stared at Isabella for a moment. I thought of using our rings to escape but Yuri and Isabella didn't have that option. Erimem nodded and turned her attention to the metal walls furthest from the doorway. She slammed her hand onto the panels over and over again until one sounded a bit different.

"This is the one," she shouted. Another round of incoming German artillery fire shook us.

The panel Erimem had thumped on didn't look any different to me but she was beating her hand on that wall, looking for something. And then she had it. A piece of wall panel swiveled revealing a little panel with buttons on it. She pressed furiously at all the controls and a second later the wall slid away. I wish she'd been wrong. Just this once.

There were four of them. Strapped to metal tables. They had been big, strong men once. They had tubes and needles stuck in them. They were still alive. They shouldn't have been and I honestly wish they hadn't been. It was like a butcher had cut into them. They'd been carved up, cut apart while they were still living. Erimem understood. We all did but none of us wanted to put it into words.

"They have been kept alive so that the flesh can be eaten fresh," Erimem said. She sounded as horrified as I felt. "They will not survive more than a few hours."

Isabella:

Lev. My beautiful Lev. Erimem was talking. I did not hear her. I saw only my husband, lying on a metal bed. His chest and one leg had been stripped of all flesh and muscle. I could see only bone in that leg. There was no flesh to cover his ribs. They had peeled his arm and one side of his face. His beautiful strong face. Worse. He was not dead. He was awake. He knew this had happened. Had he watched this thing cut him apart? Had he seen it eat his flesh? I did not know how to move. I could not. I did not know what to do. His hand moved. Veins and muscle uncovered after the skin had been peeled. I forced myself to move. Gripped the other hand. He could hardly control the movement of his eyes but he recognised me. I did not recognise his voice. The deep tone was gone. Now it was the whisper of the old when they are dying. Every word was a great effort for him. He said, "My boys." I told him they were safe, the bombs and these monsters had not touched them, and then he said this. "Get them from Russia. Far from here." An explosion shook us and he gasped in pain. The four men all cried out. It is a terrible thing to hear strong men give in to pain this way. Erimem said that the machines controlling the chemicals keeping them alive and sedated must have been destroyed. They would feel all the pain of this butchery before they died. And I remembered, what Erimem had forced into my hands earlier in the corridor. She had told me I would fight. She was wrong. My choice was worse. I felt the pistol's weight in my pocket and I gripped it. My hand did not shake as I aimed it at Lev. He could not speak. He managed only the smallest nod, but it was enough. Tom was moving to stop me but I felt the pistol jump in my hand and it was as an explosion had happened in the room with us. The shot ripped Lev's head backwards. I did not look at him. I raised the pistol again and shot each of the other men on the beds.

Andy:

She didn't move. She just held the gun out in front of her. Erimem walked slowly towards her and took the pistol from her. She stuffed the pistol into one of her pockets without speaking. She just put an arm round Isabella and pulled her to a door on the other side of this slaughterhouse. It led to a passage that twisted and turned through the ship. Isabella just stumbled on in whatever direction she was pushed. I'd seen shock like that before. It was similar to how Tom had looked. He hadn't spoken during all in that horrific place. I couldn't imagine how Isabella felt. Tom could. We hurried after Erimem.

She stopped at a round metal panel in the passage. She yanked hard on a large lever and the circular panel fell away to the outside. The freezing cold night air hit us hard and I was glad for it. It was something to distract me from what had happened. Between us we got Isabella out and we ran as fast as we could. From a good hundred yards away we watched the Russian and German shells blast the spaceship until Erimem told Yuri to get his men back. A few minutes later a huge explosion tore the ship to bits. Erimem said that something must have happened to the engines – but at least nothing would be left big enough for anyone to examine and nothing left alive inside that ship to harm anyone.

Isabella:

I remember being taken back to my home very well. But I do not know how long it took. I was there but in my mind I was not. I tried not to think of Lev or the pistol or anything I had seen in the ship. I thought instead of my boys, of my promise to their father. At my house, they did not know what to do, what to say. Yuri wanted so much to say the right words but what could he say? It did not matter. Already I was packing. I had little of any worth. Food and clothes were all I took. Blankets to wrap my children in and the money Lev had left. In the city money had been worthless for many weeks. In the country, perhaps it would have value.

Tom:

I told Erimem and Andy to stop Isabella. It was crazy. Yuri had told me that these Germans had the city surrounded. Hell, even I knew that had happened. Experiencing it was different from knowing it. I knew how it would all play out, too. The Russians would eventually break free and capture the Germans. Stalingrad wouldn't fall. The German forces would never take Stalingrad. But they didn't try to stop Isabella when she said she was leaving the city. Andy just asked if she was sure and if she knew how difficult it would be for her and for her sons. But nothing would change her mind. Erimem was actually encouraging her. Telling her which way to go. How the hell did she know anything about 1940s Russia? They were all so damn stubborn and set on Isabella leaving the city. I told him that we should take her somewhere safe with the rings but Erimem wouldn't have that. "That is not what happened," was all she said. Andy disappeared for a couple of hours and came back with food and clothes for Isabella and her boys. She had obviously been back to 2015. We made sure Yuri had some food as well. He was a good man. I liked him. I didn't know how he had survived everything he had gone through. Being honest, I don't know how I got through what I went through. One thing I was sure of – whatever had happened to me, Yuri had been through much worse. I didn't want to wonder about whether he had made it through the war. He saluted as we said our goodbyes. Isabella wasn't there.

"I am sure she'll be fine," Erimem said. "I know she will."

Isabella:

I did not see Erimem and her friends – my new friends – leave. I was already on my way from Stalingrad. I had a plan for my journey but Erimem took it from me, looked at it, said it was "Very good" and threw it on to my fire. She gave me a piece of paper. It had places, times, names of people. She said "Follow this, you will be all right."

The route she planned was so different from what I had thought to do. It made no sense. It took us along the Volga to Saratov. A cart was waiting to take us to an inn where a room and food were ready for us. The journey took many weeks. We travelled by train and boat and cart. Always there was food waiting for us, always there was money. I do not know how Erimem could do this. But I came to believe. Everything in Erimem's note was real and I believed that we would live. We travelled north, always north even though it became even colder. Penza, Tambov… we did not go into Moscow. The note told us to avoid going there. Kostroma, Konosha, Leningrad. Finally Murmansk. And there I met a man, a doctor on a ship in a British convoy, William Dunn, who tended my son Alexei when he became ill. When the time came for his ship to leave, he took us on board and did not tell his captain until we had sailed. We were married two days later by the captain. I did not love William. He did not love me. But he is a good man and he took this way to keep us safe, to give us a new home, a new country. I think both he and his captain received a great deal of trouble for their actions. I am not ashamed that we married without love. We did not think of what would come after the war. I wished to protect my boys. William had honour and chose to protect a woman and two small boys who had no other chance of life. I hated the journey at sea. I was sure hope would be stolen from us by a U-Boat so I did not dare to hope. Only when we reached the solid ground of England, I let myself think we would live. William took me to live in the home of his family. His mother was dead but his father was kind. He also was a doctor. When finally the fighting was done and he came home from sea, William and I chose to stay together. We do not have the passion I shared with Lev but William is kind, a good man. My sons are now his sons and we have two daughters. I am now a doctor's wife in a village in Kent. I bake for fetes, I help in William's surgery and I watch him play cricket. But still I remember Stalingrad and the snow and I remember Erimem.

Andy:

We saw Isabella one more time. Late at night, we stood out of view at a freezing cold docks and watched a sailor sneaking her and her boys on to a warship. I had never seen a ship up close before. They were huge. It was Murmansk. It was snowing there as well. A lot. Erimem nodded and looked pleased with herself. "I knew they would make it here safely."

She had taken no pleasure in seeing the Drofen killed. No matter what they were doing. They had been her enemy and she had given them the honourable chance to leave and they'd said no. Whatever she had done to help Isabella... she'd managed to save somebody. That mattered to her. Out of all that death, she gave life a chance.

Isabella:

My name is Isabella Dunn and I am almost ninety five years old. I have lived a good life. The years since the war have been more than I could ever have hoped for – for me, for my boys, for the daughters I had with William Dunn. My family has grown. I am now a great-great-grandmother. Though he is now almost blind, William remains as kind as the day he found me in Murmansk. I have never felt the passion for William that I experienced with Lev, but there is a different kind of love. There is friendship, companionship and trust. It is a good and honest love. I am fortunate to have loved and married two good men.

Russia is so long ago. It was a different life. I was different. The world was different. But on television when the news talked of missing professors at a University, I saw her. It was only for a few seconds. More than seventy years had passed and she was not different. He had not changed at all. I did not tell my sons or my daughters. They would think I had lost my mind. I spoke with Jacob, my grandson. The bond between us is close and has always been so. He drove me to London, to this University. Finding her was easy. She simply walked out of the University building as Jacob helped me towards it. I am not so strong on my legs as once I was and sometimes I need his arm for support. I spoke Erimem's name. She did not recognise me. I thought it was the passing of time in my face. I am so old now, but she did not know me. She was sure we had not met. But then I showed her the ring I wore on my hand. The ring she had given me in that spaceship.

Erimem:

I did not know this old woman, but as we sat together in Ibrahim's office and she told me the story of her life and of how we had known each other all those years in the past, I felt a great warmth for her. She was kind and strong. She had endured terrible things no-one should ever face and she had survived with love for her family and gratitude for the life she had lived.

I had no doubt that she knew me. She spoke of Andy and Tom. She did not know how I could not have aged but she accepted it. Stalingrad had taught her to accept many things were possible. She slowly pulled a ring from her finger and looked at it. It was one of the rings we use to travel through space and time. "You gave me this more than seventy years ago. I think it is time it was returned to you."

I accepted it. "I will give it back to you seventy years ago," I told her.

She held my hand and squeezed it. She was old and frail but that act meant a great deal to her. "Now," she said. "Long ago you shared your knowledge with me. Finally, now, it is my turn to tell you the things you will need to know."

She talked to me and took me through her memories of a cold city under siege by an enemy outside its walls and a demon within them. I began to plan my trip to the past where I would meet her for the first time..

Ibrahim:

We drove to Kent today for a ninety fifth birthday party. It's damned weird going to the birthday party of somebody you've never met. The old woman was delighted to see us. She hugged Erimem, Andy and Tom and she commented that Tom's eyes had lost some of the darkness. She was right. He looked better. He still hadn't dealt with what had happened to him but he was getting better. I heard that he had saved Andy and Isabella. The old woman thanked him for giving her all these years. That will help him. Given that we didn't know anybody there except for the old woman it was a good party. We all had a good time. Erimem gave Isabella a gift – one of the rings we use to travel. She said it wasn't the one Isabella had before. "But," she said. "It is close enough that you will not notice any difference."

We spent the afternoon at the party. It was good. There were some awkward questions to answer about how we knew Isabella but it was good. I think we needed it. We needed to see that something good could come of travelling in space and time.

Yes, it was a good day.

Isabella:

When the cold comes, I think of Erimem. I think of Stalingrad and I think of this life she gave me, and I do not feel cold.

Iain McLaughlin

ERIMEM

THE ONE PLACE

Claire Bartlett

Iain McLaughlin

If you could choose one place to go, where would it be?

That's a question you'd ask a kid. When you get older it turns into asking what you'd do if you won the lottery.

They're safe questions to ask because they're never going to happen. They're what ifs, a fantasy.

Here's the biggest what if – what if you really had the chance to go anywhere? Where would you go?

For me there was only one answer to that.

Erimem thought it was a bad idea but didn't say it in so many words. I could see it in her face, though, and she asked a couple of times if I thought it was a good idea. And she called me 'Andrea'. She only did that when she was making a point about something. Usually it was 'Andy'. It's the same way I only call her 'Your Majesty' when I'm pissed off at her.

She wasn't going to talk me out of this, and it annoyed me that I needed to ask her permission. We had all found the time travel equipment at the same time. Why did she have control of it somehow? Well, because she did. I was being unreasonable. She had travelled in time before, the equipment had come to us through people using it to try to kill her and she'd saved the universe from some kind of demon from before time or whatever people who know about demons from before time would call that kind of thing. It only annoyed me because I needed to ask her permission and I knew she didn't approve.

Having said that Erimem didn't approve, once she knew my mind was made up, she accepted that it was what I wanted and she agreed to let me use the time travel gear.

"There is only one condition," she said. "I will travel with you." And she wouldn't take any arguments on that. "You insisted upon accompanying me to Stalingrad. I will come with you now."

I didn't argue. I didn't want anyone with me but I didn't want to be on my own, either. That doesn't make sense, I know, but it's the truth.

When the time came for us to go, we kept the trip quiet. Ibrahim and Helena had gone to see a movie. I can't remember which one. I wasn't really paying attention when they were talking about it. Once they had gone we were on our way. We didn't have to change clothes to fit in. We weren't going far. Setting the co-ordinates on the control panel, I almost bottled it twice. I was more scared of this than I was of going to Stalingrad. I could persuade myself that was an adventure – or at least lie to myself and say it was. This was different.

We arrived pretty much exactly where I had planned us to appear – in the alley between the Queen Elizabeth pub and a solicitor's office. They backed on to each other and it was early morning. Nobody was around yet. The sky was starting to lighten so we were here are roughly the right time.

It was a five minute walk to the hospital. I felt sick when I saw the place. I hadn't been inside it or even walked past it since... well, that day. I remembered every corridor. The creaking door leading to the stairs was exactly as I remembered it. The signs pointing to the High Dependency Unit, too. I checked the clock on the wall. A couples of minutes yet. I pointed to a room marked "For visiting families". I knew it was empty. It always was.

Inside, there were a couple of chairs that looked like they might have been comfortable if you'd been in them for less than ten minutes, More than that and they'd hurt.

"You are here," Erimem said quietly. The door was almost closed. She was peering out through a small crack between the almost closed door and the frame. She moved a bit so I could join her.

She was right. I was there. A younger me. Not even three years ago. She was just a kid. I was just a kid. It was a different world. We had the house, cars, nice holidays. All I had to worry about was doing well at school. And I had done, too. All the A passes I wanted, my choice of universities, and then this. Mum's pain in the side. She thought it was a torn muscle or a broken rib. It wasn't either of those. When she told us it was cancer she tried to make it sound like nothing. She kept saying that most people came through cancer fine these days. She didn't sound like she believed it. She'd always been scared of cancer. Even the word got to her. Her own mum and sister had both died from it. She was an intelligent, strong woman but as soon as she got that diagnosis, she was sure she was going to die. I wouldn't say she gave up. She just didn't think it was a fight she could win. Four months later, she was here. She'd had an operation but the cancer had affected her kidneys. They weren't working and her body was poisoning itself.. Biliary sepsis, they called it. They told us she was in a bad way. I'd been sure Mum would get better. Even if she hadn't believed it, I did. I was just keeping things ticking over till she got better. When they said she needed another operation, I thought that was good, it meant they were sure she only needed the surgery to get better. Then they told us she wasn't strong enough for the surgery she needed. I didn't know what that meant. I still don't really know. But it hit me then. She wasn't getting better. I had been looking after the family for months. All the stuff about the house I hadn't worried about before because Mum and Dad did it. I did it all. Mum wasn't there and Dad was struggling to deal with what was happening. He was spending a lot of time at the hospital and a lot of the rest of his time alone. He didn't want to talk and he didn't seem able to do anything, so I did it. Cooking, washing, cleaning... I did all of that. I made sure the bills were paid. I made sure my brother went to school. I filled in for both of them because I'd been sure everything would go back to how it had been.

This was the day I knew it wasn't getting better and right now was when I realised I couldn't cope. I needed a break. I needed fresh air. I needed to not be there, just for a few hours.

Looking through that crack in the door, I saw myself stop. I sort of half raised a hand at an open door. Mum had waved at me. She had been weak. So weak. She had tubes and drips, feeding her oxygen and painkillers and god knows what. I hadn't been able to cope.

I watched myself turn and walk away. I didn't remember that I had already been crying at that point. Tears were pouring down my face. I watched myself start to run, pushing through the doors at the end of the corridor. I'd be outside in the car park, crying for a time, then I would go to the park to get a grip of myself. By the time I got home, the phone would have rung saying Mum had slipped away peacefully.

I had run away rather than sit with her for the last few hours. Dad hadn't been there either. She'd died on her own because I was too weak to sit with her. Grief is hard enough for a kid to handle without guilt keeping it company. The grief changed into something else with time, a sense of missing someone but loving the memories of the good times. The guilt didn't change. It just stayed there like a poison. It's a different kind of cancer, poisoning how you see life. How you see yourself.

I looked out of the door. The younger me was long gone. We went to the door of Mum's room. It was out of the way. They said it was for privacy. I thought they just didn't want patients seeing someone else die. She looked exactly like I remember from that night. Nothing like my Mum. Mum had always been full of life, lots of colour in her cheeks, always trying to control her weight. She lost a load of weight in just a few months and her skin looked like chalk. Actually, it looked grey. I didn't remember that from before. Her skin didn't look properly human. It just looked sick.

She *was* sick.

Her hands had been cool the last time I held them, They were really warm. Must have been the infection, I suppose. She squeezed my hand and tried to speak. She wasn't strong enough to say anything. She didn't even have the strength to be frustrated. But she was more relaxed. I'd always imagined I saw pain in her face when I left. Disappointment that I'd walked away and left her. That wasn't there anymore. She was peaceful. I talked a bit, trying to remember what I had done that day, years ago. I talked, made sure she knew how much I loved her. When she closed her eyes, I knew she wouldn't open them again. I talked some more until I was sure she couldn't hear anymore.

The quiet should have been awful. It should have hurt, knowing exactly when she would die. It didn't. I sat with her, held her hand. A nurse looked in a couple of times and checked the dialysis machine and whatever else they had her hooked to. She gave us a sad smile and asked if we needed anything before going on about her job. The quiet didn't bother me. It was peaceful. It wasn't just my Mum who had some peace. I'd felt guilty for so long that I'd run and left her to die on her own. I got to put that right.

The clock ticked round and her breathing got shallower. It was nearly time. I kissed her forehead and told her I loved her. She was already gone by then. Her body was just winding down. I was saying it for me more than for her.

When her breathing stopped we had to go. I kissed her again and let Erimem take me from the room. The nurses would find Mum in a few minutes. We couldn't be there when they came back.

Outside it was bright and sunny. Patients and staff were bustling around doing what they had to do. Erimem led me aside, to a little piece of garden mostly surrounded by bushes. She was worried. I think she was worried that I was going to start crying. Or maybe she was worried that I hadn't burst into tears already. Or maybe she understood. She had been with two of her brothers when they died, but not with her father. I think she understood.

"Are you all right?" she asked.

I was going to say that I was fine. It wasn't true but I was better than I had been. But over her shoulder I saw a familiar figure. He'd got out of our car. He took a couple of steps to the hospital then stopped. He was staring at the ground. He couldn't force himself to look at the place. He just stood there for a minute. Longer. Then he got back into the car and drove away. The way his shoulders heaved for the moment I saw him, I knew he was crying. That was the moment my father had finally broken. He couldn't cope after that. In six months he'd be gone. In a year I'd be asked to identify his body and I'd lie and say it wasn't him because I thought Matt couldn't handle losing both of them so quickly. I should have told Matt the truth. And I shouldn't have hated Dad for leaving. Losing Mum broke us. It broke him, too. He had the same guilt I did. He hadn't been able to cope.

That was when the tears came and I finally grieved. Not for Mum. For Dad. The anger and resentment didn't really matter. Not as much as him. Erimem just hugged me as tears poured down my face and every bit of grief I'd tried to hide poured out.

I found where Dad was buried and took flowers. Ibrahim and Erimem came with me. I still haven't told Matt. I don't know how to. I still don't know how he'll deal with Dad being dead. I've finally come to terms with losing my parents. Now I'm worried that's going to lose me my brother.

One thing at a time. I'll deal with Matt when it's time to. For now, saying goodbye to Dad properly is all I can do.

That one place I knew I said I would go back to… I'm glad I went. But I wish there hadn't been any need for me to go.

Iain McLaughlin

Available now from
THEBES PUBLISHING

ERIMEM

THE LAST PHARAOH

by Iain McLaughlin and Claire Bartlett
Foreword by Caroline Morris

After a freak electrical storm that seems to happen indoors, a young woman is found in the Egyptian exhibit of a London museum, and she seems to look exactly like the face on the death-mask of the uncrowned Pharaoh Erimem…

What is she doing inside the exhibit? How did she get there? Is she really a Pharaoh from 1400BC? And just who is willing to search time and space to find and assassinate her?

THE LAST PHARAOH is the first in a series of novels, novellas and short story anthologies taking Erimem, a former companion of the 5th Doctor, on a new set of adventures travelling to the past, the future and into deep space.

THE LAST PHARAOH takes Erimem and a group of 21st century students far into the past, to Actium in Greece where Erimem meets the famed Cleopatra VII on the eve of a vital battle which could end Egypt's existence as a free country and condemn it to life as a Roman province. Two great rulers of Egypt come into conflict over what Egypt needs to do in order to survive, and both Erimem and Cleopatra face their own personal battles for survival.

ERIMEM

COMING SOON

INTO THE UNKNOWN
A collection of trips into terror

PRIME IMPERATIVE
A novella by Julianne Todd

A PHARAOH OF MARS
A novel by Jim Mortimore

Available soon from
THEBES PUBLISHING

1001 COMPLETELY RANDOM DOCTOR WHO FACTS

by Claire Bartlett

Do you know when 12th Doctor Peter Capaldi was originally invited to test for the role?

Do you know who designed the Cybermen?
Or which professional teams Matt Smith played football for?
Or what links H Rider Haggard with the Third Doctor?
Or which villainous henchman was actually an opera singer?

This book is packed with 1001 facts about DOCTOR WHO, the world's longest running science fiction programme. As well as covering the TV show, there are facts about the Doctor's adventures in print, on audio, at the cinema and in the theatre. Even the most hardened fan will find there are some facts in here they didn't know about DOCTOR WHO.